In the M... ...g of America

Also by Meredith Sue Willis

Fiction
A Space Apart
Higher Ground
Only Great Changes
Quilt Pieces
(with Jane Wilson Joyce)

For Children
The Secret Super Powers of Marco

Nonfiction on Writing
Personal Fiction Writing
Blazing Pencils
Deep Revision

In the Mountains
of America

Meredith Sue Willis

Mercury House
San Francisco

Wie

This is a work of fiction. With the exception of "My Father's Stories: An Essay," names, characters, places, and incidents either are the product of the author's imagination or are used ficticiously. Any resemblance to actual events, locales, or persons, living or dead, is entirely coincidental.

"'Tis not that Dying hurts us so" by Emily Dickinson published by Harvard University Press and reprinted by permission of the publishers and the Trustees of Amherst College from *The Poems of Emily Dickinson,* Thomas H. Johnson, ed., Cambridge, Mass.: The Belknap Press of Harvard University Press, Copyright © 1951, 1955, 1979, 1983 by the President and Fellows of Harvard College.

United States Constitution, First Amendment: Congress shall make no law respecting an establishment of religion, or prohibiting the free exercise thereof; or abridging the freedom of speech, or of the press; or the right of the people peaceably to assemble, and to petition the Government for a redress of grievances.

Mercury House and colophon are registered trademarks of
Mercury House, Incorporated

Printed on recycled, acid-free paper
Manufactured in the United States of America

Library of Congress Cataloging-in-Publication Data
Willis, Meredith Sue.
In the mountains of America / by Meredith Sue Willis.
    p. cm.
ISBN 1-56279-066-8
I. Title.
PS3573.I4565515   1994
813'.54—dc20
                                                      94-13775
                                                      CIP

5   4   3   2   1
FIRST EDITION

This book is dedicated to Joel,
who is also from the mountains

"Adventures of the Vulture" appeared in *Green Mountain Review,* Spring 1994.

"The Birds That Stay" was published in *West Branch* #17, Spring 1985.

"Evenings With Dotson" appeared as "Evenings With Porter" in the *Pikeville Review,* Spring 1988.

"Family Knots" was previously published in *Kalliope: A Journal of Women's Art,* Tenth Anniversary Issue, Vol. 10, Nos. 1 & 2, Spring 1988 and in *Quilt Pieces,* Gnomon Press, 1991.

"June's Legacy" was first published as "Dreams of Deprivation" in *Fireweed: A Feminist Quarterly,* Issue 26, Winter/Spring 1988.

"The Little Harlots" appeared in *Antietam Review* (Washington County Arts Council, Hagerstown, MD), Vol. XI, Spring 1991.

"Miracle of the Locust Root" was published in *Kentucky Writing* (Somerset Community College, Somerset, KY), Vol. 6, No. 2, Spring/Summer 1991.

"My Boy Elroy," a PEN/Sydicated Fiction winner, was previously published in *Star: The Weekly Magazine of the Kansas City Star,* Sunday, September 25, 1983; in *Picture: Minneapolis Tribune,* Sunday, September 11, 1983; and in *The Available Press, PEN Short Story Collection,* Ballantine Books, Fall 1985.

"My Father's Stories" was published in *Appalachian Heritage: A Magazine of Southern Appalachian Life & Culture,* (Berea College, Berea, KY), Vol. 19, No. 2.

"To Speak Well of the Dead" appeared in *Now and Then* (Center for Appalachian Studies and Services, East Tennessee State University, Johnson City, TN), Vol. 8, No. 1, Spring 1991.

"The Trestle" originally appeared as part of the novel *A Space Apart,* Charles Scribner's Sons, 1979.

"True Romance" first appeared in *Story Quarterly 4,* Summer 1976.

Table of Contents

My Father's Stories: An Essay

CITY PEOPLE DON'T settle back when they listen to one another tell stories. In the city, it's the punch line you listen for. That was the difference I didn't catch right away. In the city, you might even interrupt the storyteller with your own quip and raise the ante. In the city, you don't settle back to listen, you lean forward.

Whereas, when my father was a boy and used to spend summers in Blackwater, Virginia, where both his parents were born, people sat *way* back. They sat in swings and on cane bottom rockers and on the porch steps. They waited for the midday heat to ease and the cornbread and bacon-boiled beans to settle. Somebody would start telling a story, and if you'd heard it already, that didn't matter anymore than it mattered that hymns and ballads were sung over. You never jumped in. You waited your turn. You might have to wait till you were a grown-up, but you knew there would be time for you too, someday, the Lord willing.

So you gazed out at the shimmer of heat between you and the

side of the unpainted barn, or maybe at a little dustcloud in the distance on the dirt road, or perhaps at the ripe tobacco in the field, and you let Uncle Eck reminisce about his time in the army in the first war. Then someone would tell about the aunt who was so pretty and smart as a button and went for a teacher, but died of influenza in 1919. Or it might be a story about finding a black snake in the bed you are supposed to sleep in.

That latter sort of story would be aimed slyly but especially at my father, who was considered a town boy, as his father had long since left the farm. My father's father, Papa Willis, had the American desire to move. He signed on as a store manager with the coal company, and they relocated him to Burdine, Kentucky; Coburn, Virginia; Owings and Shinnston, West Virginia.

But, every summer, wherever the family was, they would drive through the mountains in their Model T to Blackwater. My father tells about one of those trips. He was in a room full of relatives, he says, and Papa Willis made him stand up and turn around in the center of the room. "Now, isn't he a big one?" asked Papa Willis. "Ain't he growed big!" answered all the relatives.

"Like a big old heifer," says my father, still shaking his head fifty years later. "They stood me up and turned me around like I was a big old heifer." He doesn't mean this to be a criticism of Papa Willis, just a fact to wonder at.

To my father, Shinnston, West Virginia, represented grand new vistas. This was the great world to him in a way city people can hardly imagine. Shinnston had folks from Syria and Spain and Yugoslavia. Shinnston had a mansion on a hill built by an Italian immigrant, and a dark little shop in town where an elderly Jew repaired shoes. My father says the first day he was in Shinnston, he met Dave Hardesty, who told him: "We have a real tall man here in town named Short, and we have a little short man named Long. There's a black man named White and a white man named Black." A town of wonders: everything was possible.

My father's stories of boyhood and growing up in West Virginia have a tone of nostalgia that is missing from his visits to Blackwater. The Shinnston boyhood stories are like an intense, Technicolor version of the *Our Gang* comedies. Oh, the funny things they did. The jokes they played. Those Scotch-Irish Hardestys and black Junior Mayfield and the Italian Romeos. It seems in my father's stories that the world is populated by boys, and all the boys are equal in the rough-and-tumble of their adventuring.

There was the time they took the little billy goat up on the top floor of the Hardesty house. Well, it really wasn't such a *little* billy goat, my father says. It was really a pretty big billy goat. Papa Guy Hardesty, who owned a small coal mine, had built the biggest house in East Shinnston (but not as big as Mr. Abruzzino's mansion downtown). Papa Guy's house sat on East Avenue with the other houses. It took no commanding views, but it was very large, with a special gymnasium for the boys on the top floor.

And that was where the Hardestys and my father and the others had the goat in their circus, and also where they built the boy-sized airplane that they pushed out onto the upstairs porch, and then convinced Junior Mayfield to test pilot. Junior went on to become a career military officer, although not in the Air Force. Other times, the boys didn't choose a representative, but endangered themselves all equally; like the time they played minefield by setting mousetraps all over the gymnasium and then turning off the lights.

The Romeos had more children than the Hardestys, and less money. Mr. Romeo came over to dig coal, and to my father, the Romeos seemed the most amazing wonder of all. They always had at least one enormous bowl of spaghetti in the middle of the table for dinner, and they always elbowed out enough space for my father to join them. If the boys asked Mr. or Mrs. Romeo if he could eat with them, the adults were insulted. Of course Glenn could eat with them! He was like one of the family.

This was a kind of miracle to my father, because he was from suspicious people, people who watch you make your way up the road, across the bridge, along the path. People who give you a long, slow look before they invite you onto the porch. People who are hospitable once you're in, but don't entertain many who aren't their relatives; and they weren't always too sure what to make of a relative like my father, who lived in town.

But here were the Romeos, interrupting one another's stories, making a space on the bench, treating him as one of the clan. He loved the hubbub, the platefuls of spaghetti, the differences and the samenesses. The boys taught him to count in Italian so he could play finger number games with them. They played baseball out in the field and then football on the high school team. American boys would come up and ask how come my father played on the Eye-Tie team, and he was surprised, but unhesitating in his loyalty. He played because they were his friends, because they liked football and so did he. Because they had included him, no questions asked, for as long as he'd known them.

In his stories of young manhood, my father is the star, but still in a context of other young men. There was the time the Model T's fan belt broke, and they strapped on someone's leather pants belt to get it into town. That was the beauty of those old Model Ts, he says. Any man with a wrench could open the hood and improvise. Another time, the same car overheated, so my father and his friends peed in the radiator, enough liquid to get themselves home. You wouldn't want to run a car with that in the radiator all the time, he says, but it sure beat walking.

Or the time he and another friend, brand new teachers, went into an unfamiliar pool hall. Someone suggested a game with a little money on the side. "Sure," said my dad, winking at his friend. "Bob, do you want to go out and get our custom-made cues from the car, or shall I?"

He was always a bit of a practical joker, my father, although his greatest pleasure was the retelling and re-experiencing afterwards. Like the time he demonstrated to his chemistry class how to make table salt out of deadly sodium and chloride. It was real salt, he told the class, and to prove it, he dipped his finger in and tasted. Salt, he said. Anyone else want to try? And the student, brash and eager to be part of the show, who waved his hand, hurried up, tasted it and grinned, "Yep, you're right, Mr. Willis, that's salt, all right!"

At which point, my father seized his own throat with

both hands, gagged and bugged out his eyes, pretending to be poisoned.

HE ALSO MADE UP STORIES. I don't think he ever thought of himself as particularly creative. People from his part of the world let women make the pretty things, do most of the writing and reading. If you ask him what he is good at, my father always says, Oh, explaining things, fixing things, figuring out how things fit together.

Including stories. He used to fit together stories for me and my friends. When I was five or six, he made up one about Roy Rogers and Mighty Mouse. Actually, it was a sleazy cat villain named Oilcan Harry who my father pitted against Roy. At first, it was always Roy who would be left clinging to a cliff at the end of a segment. But over time, Oilcan Harry became the focus of the stories. When it reached the point where we were leaving Oilcan Harry in the burning shanty or tied to the rails with the train coming, I'd plead, "Oh Daddy! Please tell me how he gets loose!"

"Maybe he doesn't," he would say.

HE LIKES TO TEASE, my father. He has more than a touch of the good old country boy in his personality. I think he finds a cruel streak in this life. If anyone were to criticize his joke with the poison table salt, I think he would probably say he didn't invent meanness. Better learn about it in a safe place than out there.

Better learn to be a little mean yourself and ward it off. If you aren't alert, your cousins will put a black snake in your bed. Your chemistry teacher will pretend to poison you.

THE DAY MY FATHER graduated college, he stopped by the Romeos', still dressed in his suit, and Mrs. Romeo called him Professor. He tells this sadly, as a way of expressing something about the losses that come with growing up, about the abyss even between people who love each other.

He has another story, even less of a story, from the summers at Blackwater. One afternoon, he says, after dinner, he hid out from the field work. There was a mulberry tree at the spring where he stretched belly-down on a big cross limb. The open spring sent up breaths of coolness, and my father stuffed one big bland mulberry after the other into his mouth. "I ate them all afternoon," he says. "I ate mulberries till I couldn't squash down one single one more."

Another time, our family was driving south to visit the relatives, and he told us a story about the recent reorganization of the Hardesty mine business by Dave after Papa Guy died. It was a story about partnerships and finances, with some labor relations thrown in, and I understood almost none of it, but was soothed and stimulated by the mysteries. I listened as long as he talked.

What I want to say about his stories is that it didn't matter that I didn't understand. What mattered was the sound of the voice that seemed to unreel with the blacktop. What mattered was the wonder of the mulberries and the pain of Mrs. Romeo calling him Professor. What matters is the translucence of experience itself, which can, retold, transmit light without being entirely clear.

What I love is when the storyteller says simply, Just listen to this.

Just listen.

Listen.

My Boy Elroy

M Y GRANDMOTHER'S STORE sat at a curve in the Wise
Mountain road. It was a general merchandise store and
mail drop-off for all the farms and hollows and ridges and folds
of the mountain community of High Gap. People used to come
down near noontime and wait for the mail. The store had so
much open space that they pulled the kitchen chairs, nail kegs,
and wooden dynamite boxes near the iron stove, even in hot summer weather, just to localize the conversation.

When I stayed with my grandmother two summers in a row,
her main stock-in-trade was Pepsi Cola, pink snowball nickel
cakes, and canned lunch meat. She also sold a lot of pressed
chewing tobacco: mostly Red Man and Day's Work, which
looked like a yellow candy bar to me on some days, and like
dried dung on others. She used to have staple goods in her store,
too, bags of flour and meal, but over the years she found that the
fewer large items she sold, the less she had to enter on her credit
books; people tended to pay cash for Vienna sausages and
Dreamsicles.

The people waiting for the mail used to tell stories. I loved the slowness of the telling. I would line up coins in the coin drawer, or sit on a sack of cornmeal and look out the window, letting their voices carry me along. They took turns speaking, never interrupting each other, using short blasts of words: quick-speakers, not Deep South drawlers, but mountain talkers, rat-a-tat followed by a space. After a decent appreciative interval at the end of one story, someone else would start. I loved to be a part of those stories. Sometimes I wished I could be big enough to sit on a nail keg and take a turn, but mostly I was a little awed by the people, and happy to watch them from a distance. They had mouths that weren't like people's I knew; cheeks that had collapsed around toothlessness, and the men sometimes wore their bodies bare inside stiff blue jean overalls. The women sat with their knees apart and discreetly waved their dresses up and down for ventilation.

So I stayed at the window, or behind the counter with my grandmother. She always kept a distance herself, never joining them in the circle. People called her Mrs. Morgan, even the ones she called by their first names, and no one ever came into the living quarters in the back of the store. When I asked why, if Mrs. Robinson was a good woman, she never came back into our kitchen, my grandmother said, "Oh, honey, you have to be real careful when people owe you money."

To tell the truth, looking back, I think my grandmother's pride entered into it. She had sent her children to college, and while she didn't boast, people knew my father and my Aunt Ellen were both schoolteachers. My grandmother had a very precise line in her mind between good and bad. Educating your children and paying your bills were on the good side. Politeness was good, too, and she was polite to everyone, but she told me very clearly the difference between good people like the Robinsons who would give you the shirt off their back and the other ones you couldn't turn your back on for three seconds or they'd steal the varnish off the countertop.

And then there were the Possetts, who were in another category altogether. I first heard them mentioned in the course of someone's story around the stove. "Worthless as a Possett," someone said. I asked my grandmother later, just what is a Possett?

"Euh, euh," she said, in her special tone of humorous disgust that was supposed to make me giggle. "You stay away from those Possetts. They have cooties and they marry each other. Euh, euh."

A few days later, Earl Robinson started telling a story about the Possetts, how they'd had a fire and lost a child, or maybe two. "They never could count that good," said Earl. He paused then, and no one haw-hawed, but even I figured out the joke. "The ones that lived got burnt, too," said Earl. "All but that big Elroy. He just hightailed it out of there, didn't lift a finger to help." He went on and on, and then other people turned out to have Possett stories, too, many stories about this family that didn't have sense to pull each other out of a burning house.

One morning, shortly before my mother and father came to take me home that summer, the Possetts came to the store.

"Law, law, here come the Possetts," said my grandmother, who had gone out front to sweep the little square of cement under the step. She ran and put a piece of canvas over the bags of meal. She told me to close the kitchen door and stand by the ice cream freezer. I was not supposed to get close to them, but if any of them wanted an ice cream, I could get it out of the freezer and scoot it across the white enamel lid.

I was as excited as if they had declared Christmas in August, watching through the big plate-glass window as the Possetts came down the yellow dirt road, past the one-room schoolhouse, across the asphalt, barefooted, one after the other: two full-grown men in overalls first, the old one with no teeth and a straw hat (but, to my shame, I couldn't see that he looked all that different from a fine man like Earl Robinson), and the younger one, chubby and round-shouldered, strawberry blond. After him came the old Possett woman, who wore a boat-necked dress with no sleeves or waist, as if she had simply stitched two rectangles of fabric into a garment. The young woman had a little baby in her arms.

"Look at them," whispered my grandmother. "They think that boy Elroy is the smartest thing that ever lived. They buy him shoes in the winter and keep him fat. He got to second grade, too, before he turned sixteen and quit. I just wondered which one of them fathered that baby."

I don't understand that, I thought to myself, but I understood more than I wanted to. I tried to pay attention to the children, counting them, examining them. The little baby, plus a boy, two girls, and another boy. My stomach wrenched and I stopped counting as that last boy came across the road. He seemed to have no chin; I tried to look away. I ran to my station by the ice cream freezer, but when I turned back, the little boy was only four feet from me. He had big eyes that seemed to roll all the time because his face was pulled down by terrible stretching from his cheeks over his lower lip area. His little white bottom teeth were as exposed as a bulldog's and you could see all the healthy red flesh that should have been inside his mouth.

My grandmother said, "Is that your boy that got burned?"

Mr. Possett said, "Ee-ah," or something like that, grinning all the while, reaching behind him and grabbing the boy by the head, tugging him around for my grandmother to see. "Don't talk no more," said Possett. "Still eats, though."

My grandmother grabbed a handful of peppermint balls and maple chewies and gave them to the boy. It was as if her hands had to give to him, just as my eyes had to look. When he couldn't hold any more candy, it started dropping on the floor and the other children ran and picked it up. Mr. Possett bought himself an R.C. Cola, and after a while Elroy whined until he gave him a nickel for one, too. The mother Possett took some of the wounded boy's candy and shared it with the big girl and the baby. They sat on the kegs and boxes and looked at us, at the store. Once in a while Elroy would make a sucking noise with his R.C. Cola. Mr. Possett bought some chewing tobacco and two strips of licorice, which he tore into pieces for all the children, and then they left, back across the asphalt, up the road past the schoolhouse, into the pinewoods again.

My grandmother got a rag and wiped every wooden box a Possett had sat on, and rubbed the plate glass where a Possett had rested his cheek. She moved fast, as if she were doing something she couldn't have stopped if she'd wanted to.

I said, "What did they come down for?"

She said, "They came down to go to the store."

It was almost time for the mail; Mrs. Robinson showed up, and Mary from down the road, and, after a while, Earl Robinson. This time my grandmother did the talking, more than I'd ever heard her say to her customers. She told about the Possetts coming, about the girl with the baby big as life and Elroy fat as the hog for winter, and the boy with no chin. She went on and on, and there was no climax to her story, just the necessity of telling it.

The next summer, I didn't go down to stay by myself with my grandmother. I didn't go down until our yearly visit, and everything seemed different. My grandmother directed all her remarks to my father; she called herself an old widow-woman, and said if things got much worse she was going to end up having to marry that dirty old fellow with the greasy black hat who had the tiny store down the road. "Euh euh," she said. "He's so old and dirty. He sleeps in the same room as the store." It seemed to her, she said, that the boys nowadays were getting worse and worse, and meaner and meaner, and all the time she was getting older and feebler and more of an old widow-woman.

It didn't make any sense to me at all, because she had never looked bigger and better to me. Her hair was still brown, and she moved briskly around the kitchen, and her eyes sparkled. My father didn't take it seriously, either, and he called her by her first name. "Now, Ella," he said, the way he always did when he was being cheeky.

We were sitting around her kitchen table eating an apple pie she'd made for us from a bushel of Rome Beauties someone gave her on their bill. "You don't know," she said.

"Come and live with us," said my mother.

"You know you're always welcome," said my father.

My grandmother said, "I didn't write you about the convicts, did I? I'm getting so forgetful nowadays." My mother and father looked at each other, and then my grandmother settled in and told us about how a few weeks back, folks were sitting around waiting for the mail, and someone told about a certain Hines boy from Jenkins, Kentucky, who had broken out of jail in Pikeville. These Hineses, apparently, were the most evil-hearted bunch who ever lived. They would shoot up churches and kill off people as soon as look at them. Especially old widow-women.

"Now, Ella," said my father.

Well, anyhow, as it happened, people were worried about the Hineses coming over this way, and Earl Robinson was going to send down one of his boys to sleep in the store, but my grandmother said no, of course not, she was fine. "Well," my grandmother told us, "that very night I had this evil Hines fellow pecking at this very kitchen door. And Elroy Possett the toadstool, too."

Involuntarily, we all glanced at the door. It was a screen door to a little back porch, also screened, with a rocking chair where I loved to sit and read. She kept her brooms out there, the coal scuttle, and baskets of produce people gave her when they couldn't pay cash: the Rome Beauties, potatoes, peaches in season, and more tomatoes than she could ever eat. This porch had a door and three steps down to the garage and coal house.

The thing that frightened her that night, she told us, was that the knocking was on her back door instead of at the store door.

She had been watching Bret Maverick on television when she heard it, and she walked into the kitchen without turning on the light because she had a bad feeling and wanted to look at who was knocking before they saw her. She passed the telephone, thinking all the time she should call the Robinsons, but she didn't want her imagination running away with her. She didn't want to act like a timid old widow-woman, even if she was one.

"So," she said, "I ended up with convicts at my back door and no help but myself."

"Come and live with us, Mother," my father said, not fooling around now.

"And do what? Set in a chair? No, I'll just keep on working and getting deeper in debt till some convict really does get me."

She had stood in the dark kitchen, peering at the shape on the steps, pressing at her outer door. No friendly voice saying, Hey, Mrs. Morgan. Nothing she could recognize as a Robinson or an Otis. The television was still going in the background, cowboys shooting. She made out another man down on the ground at the bottom of the steps, and at a little distance, by the garage wall, a cigarette ash glowing. Three of them, she thought, and that was when her blood ran cold. Three men, and she was sure they were convicts. She spoke suddenly, harshly, as if the force of her voice could blow the man off her steps. "What do you want?"

"You the store lady?" he asked, without so much as a *good evening*.

"Store's closed," my grandmother answered, working on a plan in her mind. What she wanted to do was ease herself over to the telephone and gently give a message to the Robinsons. It was a party line, and with luck one of the girls would be on the phone already, talking to her boyfriend. She had heard the Robinson's ring just a little while before, and she thought she might be able to whisper that she needed help without these convicts hearing her over the television. "Store's closed, boys," she said again.

The fellow pressed his shadow face into the screen wire, trying to see. He gave a slimy little laugh, and she thought she could smell whiskey. "Aw," he said. "We was wanting something, too."

"Who's we?" said my grandmother. "Do you think I open up to every Tom, Dick, and Harry?"

The snicker again. "I don't think you know us, ma'am." She knew he could break the little hook and eye on the door in no time, and once he did that, once he started breaking her things, she would have lost the chance to do anything but scream.

A voice came from the cigarette glow. "Tell her to give us a drink of water, Ed." She was sure the one staying back so far was the leader. He was the Hines. The dangerous one with his picture in the paper, standing back out of sight.

The third one, the big hulk, at the bottom of the stairs, said, "Naw, you said I could have a R.C. Cola to drink."

My grandmother said, "Elroy Possett, is that you down there?"

A snuffle and a giggle. "Yes, ma'am."

Well, my grandmother saw it all in a flash then. She saw the convicts running across Elroy, who was probably sitting on a rock by the side of the road, and them asking him who had money around these parts, and him saying, Oh, Mrs. Morgan, she owns a big store.

"That's how dumb the Possetts are," my grandmother told us.

"The most money they can think of is me and my poor little in-debt store with nothing but books full of credit." She said it made her so mad to think that Elroy Possett had got her in all this trouble that she threw the light switch, jut hit the whole bunch of them with the spotlight my father had installed so she wouldn't stumble going out to load her coal scuttle. Light all over Elroy, who shaded his eyes. The fellow up on the steps already had a hat pulled low over his eyes, and the one down by the garage stepped back in the shadows, so she never did get a look at him.

"Now, why'd you do that?" said the one called Ed, and my grandmother took a closer look at him; narrow-shouldered, with clothes that didn't fit, like they belonged to another man. Like they'd been stolen, she thought.

"Tell her what we want, Ed," said the man in the shadows.

"Well," said Ed, "we was travelling and we got hungry and this fellow here said you could sell us some lunch meat and bread and pop."

While he talked, my grandmother kept looking at his hat, a man's regular dress hat of a greasy black color, and it reminded her of something, and all of a sudden she was sure it belonged to the old fellow with the little store about a sixth the size of her own. She thought, Lord Lord, they killed that old man who wanted to keep me company, they killed him and took his money and his hat and now they're going to kill me. It was the hat that set her imagination to working. She wasn't the kind of person to imagine out of nothing, but the hat and the grease spots made her see the old bristle-chinned fellow lying with his throat cut in a pool of blood in that store, where, if his head was at the stove, then his feet must be out the door. She saw her own blood then, too, on the linoleum of her kitchen floor. Saw her apron and her plaid print dress. Saw a terrible stillness of sunrise on herself laid out on the floor with no life in her.

She heard another snuffle from Elroy, and it infuriated her that a filthy oaf like Elroy Possett was going to be the death of her. She got so mad, she snarled, "What are you laughing at, Elroy Possett? It isn't funny these poor boys being hungry and thirsty in the middle of the night like this and wanting a little something, and you know very well I can't open up this store."

"Yes, ma'am," said Elroy.

The one named Ed with the old man's hat said, "Just some lunch meat, lady."

"Can't open the store," she said. You know I'm not one to have wild ideas, she told us; it was something about the Possett that gave her the idea. "I can't open my store, much as I'd like to."

The man in the dark said, "And why's that, ma'am? We surely would like a little something to eat."

My grandmother kept looking at the Possett, the only one of that whole family with any meat on him, no doubt stealing from his mother and the little ones, no doubt giving his sister that baby. She said, "Elroy Possett knows why, don't you Elroy? I can't open up because of my boy Elroy."

There was a little silence, and Elroy Possett said, "Yes, m'am."

She said, "You know all about my poor Elroy, don't you?"

Ed said, "What are you talking about?"

Elroy Possett said, "Her boy Elroy."

"How many Elroys *is* there around here?"

"Two of us," said Elroy Possett, and my grandmother's head began to swim. Some moths and beetles were flapping and flying and banging on the spotlight, and the one named Ed slapped at them.

"Tell us about him," said the one in the dark.

"He's a bad boy," said Elroy Possett.

"Now, Elroy," said my grandmother, feeling a kind of joy; things happening, and she wasn't still yet. "Now, Elroy, don't talk about my poor boy like that. He never hurt me."

"He hurts other folks, all right."

The one down in the shadows said, "Where is this fellow? I'd like to see this Elroy."

"Law," said my grandmother. "I'd never disturb him."

"Don't disturb him!" said Elroy. And my grandmother turned out to have underestimated him, because it was Elroy Possett who made up the next part. "That Elroy sets in the store next to the money box with a shotgun, and nobody never gets near nothing."

Ed cursed. "Why the———"

"Blank," my grandmother said.

"Why the blank did you bring us here then?"

Elroy Possett was having a good time; his imagination was working away. It must have been a real treat for him, said my grandmother, to feel his brain working.

"Yes, sir, that Elroy sets right there with that shotgun and blows folks' heads off. He sleeps in the daytime and shoots burglars at night. He shot lots of burglars."

My grandmother was getting worried that Elroy was going to ruin it by saying too much. "Now, Elroy, you're exaggerating." "Why ain't he in jail?" asked Ed.

"Well, he never killed anybody," said my grandmother. "He has real bad coordination, my boy Elroy. He never hurt those boys, the time Elroy's talking about. They wasn't supposed to be in the store, after all. The sheriff agreed to that."

The one down in the dark said, "Tell him to step aside then, ma'am, he'll do what you tell him."

"Law no," said my grandmother. "I'm sorry to say that I'm not a trusting woman. I have a suspiciousness in me."

"Let's go," said the one in the dark, and the cigarette went hurling off. "She ain't letting nobody in her store."

Elroy Possett said, "That Elroy is ugly too. And he ain't bright."

Ed cursed again, then cursed Elroy and stomped down the steps, and Elroy went after him. My grandmother said she went around checking all her window locks, then she got out the butcher knife and sat all night in the kitchen with the knife in her lap.

"Why didn't you call the Robinsons?" asked my mother.

"It was getting late," my grandmother said. "Besides, I always like to do what I can by myself."

"We're getting you a gun," said my father.

"I'd shoot my foot. Beside, it turned out those Hines boys got caught earlier that day all the way over in Danville. Those boys weren't the convicts after all," she said. "Although I do believe they were mean as convicts."

I asked, "What about that hat?"

She shrugged. "Two hats. The old man was fine. I got a message from him the next day through the bread boy. He wanted to take me out for a drive on Sunday. In my car."

"Just the same," said my father, "we're getting you a gun."

"All I need," said my grandmother, "all I need is for people to pay their bills."

"Did Elroy come back?" I asked her. "Did you ever see him again?"

"Of course," said my grandmother. "He brought the whole family down again a day later. The whole defective mess of them. They stood around my store for three hours and never bought a thing."

She looked at us. "Do you know what they were waiting for?"

I knew, but I said, "What?"

She gave a nod with her chin. "They were waiting to see my boy Elroy."

The Birds
that Stay

'Tis not that Dying hurts us so—
'Tis Living—hurts us more—
But Dying—is a different way—
A Kind behind the Door—

The Southern Custom—of the Bird—
That ere the Frosts are due—
Accepts a better Latitude—
We—are the Birds—that stay.

The Shiverers round Farmers' doors—
For whose reluctant Crumb—
We stipulate—till pitying Snows
Persuade our Feathers Home.

—Emily Dickinson #335

Lisa

MY MOMMY IS GONE. My grandma says and my grandpa says and my great grandma Ella says: My Mommy is gone to a better place because God needed good people to be beautiful there. He took her in her Eastern Star dress and a blue scarf on her head because God took her hair already. She went to heaven in the red wagon three times around the house and then I buried her, I mean, the ladybug. I dug the hole and buried the ladybug with dandelion flowers. More flowers than any other ladybug ever had. The bug climbed right up the dandelions and flew away.

There was a bug flying up in the air at church, too, and I said to Grandpa, There goes my mommy!

Ma Ella Morgan

LOSING JODELL HAS BEEN a hard thing for all of us, but it doesn't make what's wrong right. Jody Otis is a good man, but I know what he has planned in his mind. I don't care what Jodell's husband did, what Jody is planning is wrong.

For years I haven't thought about how I didn't want my Ellen marrying Jody Otis. He's been so good to her, and good to me. "Ma Ella," he told me, "I don't have my own mother anymore, and next to her I never respected a woman more than you, so you know you always have a home with Ellen and me." And he meant every word of it. The Otises were always like that. Loyal people, the best people ever lived to those they love.

But if you cross them.

I see him here today with his hands on his knees sucking in air like poison phlegm, and I remember what else I know about the Otises. They weren't bad boys like some families; even the meanest one of them went for a preacher in the end, and I say more power to him. But they all had a way of lining things up like dominoes. Something old-timey about the Otises. That was why I told Ellen to go and marry someone from the college, but she liked the way Jody stuck by her. He was going overseas in 1942 when she got the telegram. She hadn't had a letter from him in four months, and then here's this telegram saying, COME TO THE NEW YORK CITY HOTEL.

I said, "Don't you dare get on that train; that boy didn't say a word about getting married and that don't even sound like the name of a real hotel."

So Ellen started crying and we had the biggest mess because she was softhearted and couldn't bear to go against me, but all the time she was packing her suitcase. She kept saying, "If I don't go, Jody wouldn't understand." Well, she was right about that. That's the way the Otises are. They expect their people to come when they call. My poor baby girl Ellen had the devil's own time finding him. There wasn't any New York City Hotel, or any rooms in any other hotels, and she had to get the military police and everyone else out looking for him. But it all worked out, and they got married, and he's done real well, I have no complaints about that. He keeps a store and does a little farming, but smart farming, not dirt farming like his Pap. Some big company delivers him a couple thousand little peeper chickens and he raises them for six weeks in a shed behind the house, and then the company comes and buys them off him for fryers. He and Ellen have five automobiles, and that not counting tractors and the riding lawn-mower. He has his pickup truck and the four-wheel drive for hunting and Ellen's little Chevette and the big champagne-colored Lincoln Continental, and then there is that red Corvette car he bought for Jodell.

To tell you the truth, I always thought the Corvette would kill Jodell. Here she was, a young married woman with a baby of her own and a job teaching and she was driving up and down these narrow mountain roads in that topless red thing. I don't know why her husband Buddy let her do it. I don't know why Ellen let Jody get it for her. But all Jody knew was his Jodell wanted it and Buddy couldn't afford it, but Jody could, so he did. That's the way the Otises are.

I used to fall into a little nap sometimes and I would jerk awake thinking that car was going over the side of the mountain. I would see it hanging in midair and Jodell's hair flying in the air behind it. Somehow I never believed the cancer could kill her, I was so sure of that ugly red car. I still forget sometimes, when they say, Oh, Mrs. Morgan, what a sad thing, to lose your grand-daughter to cancer, and I almost say, every time, What do you mean? She died when her car went over the mountain.

And if the cancer played some evil joke and cheated the Corvette car, then what gave Jodell cancer was that she never ate right. She was a good child, but willful, that's how Jodell was. More Otis than Morgan. Many times I told her to her face she didn't eat right, but she'd always say, "Oh, Ma Ella, you just want everybody as fat as you and Mama." She was full of life and had a smart mouth, but never meant anything by it. We tend to run to flesh in our family, so Jodell lived on those Diet-Rite Colas and little tiny frozen Weight Watchers dinners. She kept herself slim, most of the time. It was like she couldn't bear to set her weight down on this earth, the way she dieted and hopped around all the time. Ran all over creation in that car. I can't help thinking that if she'd had more flesh in the first place, she wouldn't have wasted away so easy.

Eating good is coming back, too. I hear them talking about it on Phil Donahue, and even old Merv Griffin had on some actress who turned into a nutrition woman. The way she talked about eating all vegetables, it sounded to me like the kind of country meal I was raised on: corn and tomatoes and green beans, boiled up with a little bacon grease was the way we always cooked them. Ellen served that kind of food, too, and Jody always kept a garden, so there was plenty of good food on their table. Make that child eat right, I said to Ellen, but Ellen said, It's too late now, Jody spoiled her. I've seen her put a meal on the table and Jodell say in this little whiny voice, I don't like that. I'd say, Then don't eat it, but Jody would say, And what does my baby feel like eating? And she'd say, Pizza or Chicken-in-a-Basket, and he would pick her up from the table and take her to the drive-in and leave me and Ellen sitting there. I don't mean to say he didn't bring us back some pizza, too, but it like to broke my heart, a hot meal on the table and him taking that child out for pizza and french fries! He spoiled her like she was a little piece of candy he was trying to make last, but it melted in his pocket after all.

I don't mean to be hard on Jody, but he hates better than he loves. And I do mean to watch him. I know what he's thought of. He keeps a gun in that pickup truck of his. Jodell and Buddy had their troubles, but so did Jody and Ellen—and so does everyone else, I'll tell the world. But the Otis in him wants to pay back somebody because he lost Jodell, and the best one he sees to blame is Buddy. Buddy is grieving worse than the rest of us, but Jody won't admit it.

What I've been thinking about as I sit here is what I'm going to do if Jody up and goes for his gun. I can't get my knees locked into position fast enough to stand in his way, but I might be able to say something. First, I thought of quoting scripture, *Vengeance is mine saith the Lord;* but I never have been the kind of woman who quotes Bible. Then I thought of reminding him of his mother, but those Otis women were as bad as the boys for paying back what's owed. I might try saying how Lisa will be an orphan, but I think he'd rather have her an orphan than have Buddy for a parent.

So what I have planned is, when he starts out for his gun I'm going to shout his name first, good and loud: Jody! And then I'm going to say, Don't you know it wasn't Buddy who killed Jodell, it was you? You spoiled her to death.

Jody Otis

I watch the feet. The pair I look at most is in the kitchen, passing the doorway from time to time, the feet of the pit viper. I look at the soles on the shoes he wears, and I'm glad those soles are thick and keep his feet off my kitchen floor, because I despise the ground he walks on.

If I had ten daughters, or five daughters and five sons, or even if I had one more daughter ... But I never imagined I would outlive Jodell. Sometimes I am afraid I'll be the last of all my people: my parents are gone, and my brother Barron in the war and Ansel in the mines. No one left but me and Ed and Dwina, and Ed coughs all the time and Dwina looks bad to me. Sometimes I look around and see people going and it's like leaves on the trees in the fall. A few of the oak leaves still hanging there, but such a dead color of brown.

Being in the world without Jodell isn't natural. Parents going first, and one brother before another, that's natural. But it's not natural that Jodell is gone. When Lisa comes up yelling Grandpa, I see Jodell's face. I see her standing in the corner hide-and-seeking me. I see her jumping off the side of the porch like steps weren't made for her. Daddy! Daddy! she yells. Mama wants a big loaf of white bread, not a little one, and can I come to the store with you? Well, hop in, I say.

When she first went down to college, I thought I'd die of loneliness, but she came home every weekend, and she told me all about it. She told me who kissed her, and when she thought she was in love with this one and that one. And then it was the same one, coming up on weekends with her, and the next thing I knew she was talking about marrying him.

I never guessed either. I never noticed the shape of his head or the little pinholes behind his eyes. I thought it was like the old folks say, I wasn't losing a daughter, but gaining a son. Oh, that boy ate up country living. He was from town, but he always felt out of place down there, he said. Always knew inside he was a country boy. He carried groceries for Ellen before I could get to it, and he kept up on Ma Ella's soap operas and talked to her longer than it was natural for a young man to do. He was dying for me to take him coon hunting, he said, and how he wished his own father was like me. I keep seeing his face in my mind, paying me those poison compliments. Sometimes I can't see Jodell's face for seeing his.

For a long while she did everything with us, too. She even went hunting with us. She would clean his squirrels when he shot them, even though she always told me she couldn't stand the insides of animals. When she got pregnant, she couldn't go out so much, and she got mad. I can see her mad, all right: one hand on her hip and her head to one side. "Daddy!" she says, real exasperated. "Daddy, I wouldn't mind fighting some woman for him, but I never thought I'd have to fight you!"

Oh, Jodell, my baby. I laughed. Him and me laughed together, me and the pit viper. The way my brothers and I used to tease Dwina. I get cramps in my stomach thinking I was ever with him against Jodell, even for half a minute, even for fun.

She came to me, though, when she found out. She came straight to me. She said, "Daddy, he's going out on me. I know he is." I was going to horsewhip him, I was going to bust his face, but she wouldn't let me go. She clung to me like she did at the end, hung on till I slowed down. I got out the door and down the steps before she stopped me. She was crying and saying, No no, and I stopped. If I'd knowed then what I know now, if I'd knowed she was already injected with his poison, I wouldn't have stopped.

And my wife, Ellen, who is a good woman, a Christian woman, wants me to forgive the rattlesnake. She keeps working at me, saying, Oh Jody, look how that poor boy Buddy suffers ... Oh, look how good he was to her in the hospital ... Oh, look at him cry. She says, Forgive him, Jody, like a Christian man. And in my heart I say, I was a man first and a Christian after, and I will not forgive him. I am going to send his soul to hell, if those women don't keep me from it.

The way I see it is, I'll go to hell, too, but it's worth it. The way I see it is him and me both in the flames. I see the flames coming, a big flash-flood wall of acid and flames rolling down this dry riverbed. He's up on the bank, out of sight of the flood, and I wave and grin like the awfullest old hypocrite of a lay preacher that ever was, and I say, Hey Buddy! Hey Buddy, come on down here and let me show you something! And he slides down the bank and trots right over to me, and I put an arm around his neck and swing him about-face, just in time to get a good look at what's coming at us. It hits us together then, rolls us over, and I feel the heat in my throat choking me, but at the same time I'm so satisfied. I'm willing to go to hell for that satisfaction.

I mean to trail him when he's with one of his girlfriends. I'll let him go in her house, and I'll watch the lights go out and let him do his evil one more time, now that Jodell can't be poisoned by it, and then I'll wait with the shotgun by his car. I want to blow his face off. I want him to have no nose and no eyes when the world ends and people come up out of their graves.

They say it's the same as a battlefield then, at the end of the world. They say there's a low evil strip of sunset and trees all blasted to stumps and heavy black clouds. They say you can't tell the clouds from the smoke hanging over everything and you don't know when some devil's going to jump you. Then the mud begins to turn over like a plough passing through it, and they all come up, strangers and folks that might be your relatives, in old-fashioned suits and long dresses, and men with holes in their hearts. And then *he* comes up with his face like the insides of a dead squirrel, and she comes in her blue dress, and she runs right by him, even though they be buried side by side. She doesn't recognize him, either, she comes yelling Daddy! Daddy! What's going on here?

And I say, I don't know, but I'm here with you, Jodell.

If I don't shoot him, it will be because of the women working on me. All these church ladies putting food on my knee and Ma Ella staring. And Ellen asking me to run out to the garden and pick a beefsteak tomato and Lisa putting her hands on her hips and her head to one side, just like Jodell, saying, "Grandpa, where *is* my mommy?"

If I don't kill him, that pit viper's mother can thank the old women and children.

I guess she can thank Jodell, too. "Don't you dare touch him," Jodell said. "He's mine and he'll be mine even after I'm dead." I don't know if I believe that, but I suppose if Jodell wants him alive with his remorse, then I won't deny her.

Ellen Morgan Otis

I DON'T WANT TO FEEL any bad feelings. I want to grieve for my dead daughter, Jodell, and feel love for all these fine people here today grieving with us. I want to remember the words the preacher said about her, and in my mind I want to see her rising to the right hand of God with organ music, trailing clouds of glory. I want to grieve and love like a Christian woman, and to be thankful.

I want to feel thankful for the simple, kind things, like these three hams and four bowls of potato salad and four angel food cakes. For the two pans of fried chicken, the meatloaf, and the raisin pie. I want to feel thankful for the flowers, too, six baskets more than for any other funeral he ever had, the undertaker told me. Flowers from the other teachers, from her students at school, her Sunday School class and her college sorority and the Eastern Star—and on and on. Beautiful masses of all kinds of flowers.

My daughter Jodell had a beautiful soul and she was loved. That was the way the preacher said it, and I don't think there was a dry eye in the church.

People keep trying to get me to eat. I haven't been paying any attention to my diet, and I hardly notice whether or not I eat, but I do know they keep setting plates in front of me. I can turn down the ham and chicken, but something in me is hungry for the white foods: the potato salad and especially the angel cake. I could never turn down a slice of light angel cake with that little bit of brown stickiness on the crust. I pick at a crumb off the side, but then someone starts talking to me and, the next thing I know, the plate is empty and I have that comforted, full feeling inside. But the good feeling doesn't last. It starts to expand out against my girdle, like indigestion. A sort of sick, swelling feeling. And then—I'll be in the middle of talking to someone—I suddenly remember, like a little burp: Oh! Jodell's dead. And all the hungry emptiness is back, like I never ate a thing, and I start crying.

But we made the funeral everything Jodell wanted, and almost everything she asked for. She chose the dress herself. She said, "Now, Mama," and this was before she went in the hospital the last time, "Now, Mama, if it comes to it, I want to wear the light blue formal with the scoop neck and I want my hair lying loose on the pillow. I don't want some old stiff hairstyle. I want to look like I always do." Well, my poor child didn't have any hair by the time the doctors had done what they could with the drugs, and the funeral director suggested a wig, but everything he showed me was so stiff, that I said, no, I thought I would just use the blue silk scarf Buddy got her. Some folks thought it was unusual for the deceased to wear a scarf, but I believe it was what she would have wanted.

Everything was just as close to the way she would have wanted it as was humanly possible, even though it wasn't easy. When they put the dress on her, they had to call me because it was standing out from her body like a circus tent. My family has always been heavyset, and even Jodell had a little bit of a figure, especially after Lisa was born, but she lost sixty pounds with the cancer. Where did sixty pounds come from? It was such a shock to see the dress standing there by itself, five inches off her body. The funeral director suggested some bodices he had, or her favorite blouse, but I said no, I couldn't give her back her hair, but I could at least send her to earth in her favorite gown. Mother and I stayed up most of the night sewing it by hand. We cut out the zipper and the whole back, so they could slip it over her without disturbing things, and I couldn't just leave the back edge raw, without a hem. Then we decided to take out the boning, so it wouldn't stand up over her bust, and Mother, with arthritis in her hands, insisted on whipstitching blue satin over the inside; we wanted that dress finished right, inside and out.

And everyone said she looked lovely. I go over and over it in my mind, each little detail: the flower arrangements, the obituary they read over the radio. It's surprisingly like a wedding, when you think about it. How you want everything just so. I tried to do it all to please Jodell. I might have had them put a wig on her for myself, but I tried to do what she would have preferred, even if people talked behind my back.

I always try to please people. Mother says it's my best and worst quality, that I let people walk all over me sometimes. I try so hard, and that's why it seems cruel that I don't have only loving thoughts at a time like this. I keep thinking so many things I wish would be buried with her. Bad thoughts against my own daughter dead of cancer and buried this day.

All of Jody's bad thoughts are aimed at Buddy. The poor boy sits here, so pathetic, in the kitchen with the women because Jody turned the men against him. Jody is wrong, too. Whatever Buddy did to Jodell, he's paying. The whole year she was sick, that boy was stricken. He acted like she was the sun rising and setting. He kissed her fingers and cried in her lap and begged her to forgive him. He bought her bed jackets and silk scarves, and she wouldn't let anyone else—not the nurses, not me—give her a sponge bath. I'll never forget the sight of that big boy on his knees with tears running off his cheeks into the pan of water, sponging off what was left of her arm, finger by finger, then the wrist, and up to her elbow. Sobbing like his heart would break. And her smiling all the time. "Look at him, Mama," she said. "Look how good he treats me."

The thing was, and dear Lord forgive me for saying it, she seemed to be enjoying herself. Enjoying having Buddy at her feet like that. Getting her way.

I'll give Lisa a kiss, such a doll baby, her grandma's sugar. Not many children have their grandmother and their great grandmother both, even if they have to lose their mother. She makes me think of Jodell at that age, of course, so pretty and chubby. That much is easy, to have all good thoughts. I'll try to think of Jodell as a little girl in a place of light, where we'll all be together someday, with shining and music and nevermore to part.

I start out seeing her there, and then I hear her voice as brittle as china, saying, "Mama, if it's true Buddy is going out on me, I couldn't walk into school." "Why sure you could, honey," I say, "*you* haven't done anything wrong. Buddy's the one who's wrong, if anybody is." "No," she says, "it hasn't got anything to do with right and wrong, it's got to do with me not being able to walk into Daddy's store or the school knowing people were talking behind my back. I'd die first."

I hear that in my mind and have this evil thought, to blame her for dying. She acted as if she was the only person who ever lost anything. As if nobody ever before was disappointed in life. Mother says that's what life is all about, anyhow, that everyone starts out dewy fresh and hoping, and every step of the way gets disappointed till they dry up and wither away. Nobody ever guessed that I lost Jody. He said it to my face, he said, "Lord, Ellen, I never loved anything like I love Jodell." He never thought he was hurting me. He never *meant* to hurt me, never guessed how much that hurt me. The worst of that kind of hurting is that it causes other bad feelings: it caused me to be jealous of my own child, which is wrong and evil if anything ever was wrong and evil. And when I finally thought I had it beat, when Jodell was on her deathbed, it came back to me.

I was actually afraid sometimes it was my evil feeling making her sick. I was all loving on the outside and full of that nastiness on the inside. I asked God to make me *simple,* just a plain ordinary mother who was losing her child, but I was two-faced in secret, not a good woman, when all I ever wanted in this world was to be good and do right.

I remember one particular afternoon when Jody drove fifty miles to a place where we used to get hot dogs with a real good chili sauce. Jodell had been lying in the hospital bed with all of us around her, reminiscing and saying how, even though nothing tasted good to her, she kept remembering those delicious chili dogs and how they used to hit the spot. And Jody, he never said a word, although I knew what he was doing, he just got up and left the hospital and drove fifty miles to bring her what she wanted. She sat there like an angel, propped on her pillow, no more able to eat that chili dog than anything else, just dipping the tip of her tongue in the sauce, saying, "I'm eating it, Daddy. Look, I'm eating it." And Jody and Buddy on either side of her with their faces turned away crying. And my bad heart inside me saying, What a satisfaction to that girl to see those two men cry!

I think it must be hardest of all to be left with your own bad heart. Hardest of all to know that, in spite of the flowers, in spite of doing what you know she wanted, and in spite of loving her, you had bad thoughts. To be afraid you killed her with bad thoughts. But I know that isn't true, and it isn't true that Buddy killed her with hurt, or Jody killed her with love. She just died. God took her for his own reasons, and that's the only thing given us to know.

I sit with darkness on one side of me like a chasm and all that's good and beautiful on the other side like an enormous chrysanthemum. I am in the middle. Yes, I say, It's an unknown mystery. We do not know, we do not know.

The Little Harlots

ONE HOT INDIAN SUMMER morning when he was fourteen, Roy Critchfield stood on the deserted strip mine road, looking down at the back of Reverend Robinette's house. He was full of rage. His father said that if a man isn't kept in check, he'll blow a gasket, and at this moment, Roy could feel the pressure building.

Usually he did pretty well at holding himself in, the way his father said a man had to. He had Methods. One was to roll up his sleeves and gaze for a long time at his arms and the new black hairs sprouting at irregular distances, and at the straight, heavy length of his arm bone. He knew he had almost a man's strength now, and thinking about his strength helped.

His other method was to keep good-sized, creek-bed stones in his pockets at all times. The stones were his special protection against the little harlots, so he even took them to bed, to keep his hands clean when they came in rows, in ranks, with round breasts and wide hips and tiny waists like Delilah in the first movie he ever saw. Roy's father hadn't even allowed his mother to see that movie, but he took Roy by foot to their town, Viola, and then by bus to Clarksburg and the Robinson Grand Theatre. Roy never forgot Delilah's swishing skirts and jeweled naked waist. She stayed with him when nearby things like homework and weeding the garden slipped away. The little harlots were a dream of Delilah, glowing in Technicolor and multiplying and coming to him as he lay in bed at night, sweating and swelling like Samson in chains. Sometimes, when they had done all they could, and he had either kept himself chained or else lost his strength and given in to them, they rang little bells and lay down to sleep beside him. Sometimes, Roy would lie back down, too, and sleep through his alarm clock, especially now that his mother wasn't around to call him for school.

It had been a terrible and eventful four months, and it felt to Roy as if nothing would ever be ordinary again. His mother had left home, and the little harlots had started to come in daylight. He gazed down at Reverend Robinette's yard and thought it was unnatural too since the arrival of Mrs. Robinette. There were white wrought-iron furniture with flowery plastic pillows and geraniums in pots along the retaining wall. The sheer number of potted plants deepened Roy's anger: potted plants belonged *inside* a house. His mother always kept an African violet in her kitchen, but it had one blossom at a time, the opposite of this flood of red, pink, and white, dropping their crumpled old blossoms, their yellowed leaves, untidy and profuse.

Roy thought that if Mrs. Robinette had never come to live with Reverend Robinette, his mother's violet would still be at home in the kitchen. If Mrs. Robinette had not come, the Big Haul Full

Gospel Church would still be one church, instead of the big church over here and the separate smaller one that met in Roy's father's tractor barn with Wayne Wade as the preacher.

Wayne's church didn't believe in instrumental music. Make a joyful noise, Wayne said, means with your mouth and throat, not with a piano. Wayne said that Mrs. Robinette had a college degree in piano playing and church music, and she intended to use it come hell or high water, and it looked like it was going to be hell. Now that she had turned the head of Reverend Robinette and most of the church members and gotten a piano in there, they'd forgotten the *simple* Gospel, praise Jesus. They might just as well close the precious Bible, Word of God, and let it gather dust.

Wayne had been the lay preacher of the Big Haul Church before they raised the money to build the new church and hire a regular ordained minister. Reverend Robinette's popularity had expanded the church; the Sunday evening services, especially, had drawn young people from all over town. Often, after the evening service, if it was still light, they used to get up a game of baseball, and that was when a couple of the town boys asked Roy to come down and try out for the summer league. Roy had asked Reverend Robinette if he thought that was all right, and he never could quite remember what Reverend Robinette had said about baseball that first time. Maybe nothing, but certainly not a flat out no, because Roy hiked into town the very next day and started to play.

His big-knuckled fingers seemed to have come knowing how to slip over a ball; he had a natural aptitude for throwing, although on the rare occasions when a ball was hit and came back to him, he had a lot of trouble remembering what to do with it. Still, it was the first time he'd had a natural aptitude for anything. He did passing well in school, but it always took an effort to keep his mind on blackboards. The wonderful thing about pitching was that it was almost as if he threw without getting his mind involved at all. His best pitch was a sidearm that surprised him as much as it surprised the batter: it seemed to burst out of nowhere like a sunburned freight train. The coach said all he had to do was straighten it out a little, and it could be the pitch of the century. So Roy prayed for straightness. Not for a strike, or to win the game, but for straightness. He prayed for the purity of a pine tree's shaft, and it was the pine tree's shaft he wanted to throw.

If it had been only the straightness and the speed, there might have been no conflict, but Roy began to love the esteem of his teammates. Boys who used to call him High Pockets when he went into Viola now said, "Whoo, Old Roy threw a scorcher that time! Old Roy burned them good!" And he'd break into a sweat and his head would swell too heavy to hold up, and he'd feel his whole self melting toward some kind of spineless babyhood that he never wanted to stop. Sometimes, to his amazement, he pitched even better after these moments of melting. This was like a miracle to him, but even more of a miracle was when they asked him to go out after the game.

He had never had a bunch of friends before; he'd never learned to hang out. He had been, for all practical purposes, an only child, his mother's change-of-life baby, his nearest brother thirteen when he was born. No kids lived nearby that he was allowed to play with. All the kids up Big Haul, according to his father, chewed tobacco, had dads who were drunks, and cursed to beat the devil.

So, the miracle was how his teammates would buy him a hot dog and a coke at Tubby's Luncheonette, even though he never found anything to say, and how they still seemed to think he was one of them, and he could listen as long as he liked while they retold their game, talked about the Pittsburgh Pirates and the New York Yankees. And Roy would have flashes of insight about when it was best to throw to first base and when to second.

But he never opened his mouth to ask the boys not to take the Lord's name in vain, and he never once asked even one of them if they'd been born again. The real problem was, he didn't want to ask them. What he wanted was to do just what he was doing: sit among them, listen, laugh, eat hot dogs, drink cokes.

HE HAD COME OVER the hill the back way looking for Reverend Robinette, who was still a bachelor at the time. He knocked at the sliding patio doors, and Reverend Robinette called him into the bedroom, where there was a suitcase full of socks and shirts, and he was just tying his tie. "Roy," he said. "You barely caught me. I was about to go away for a couple of days."

When a thing was on Roy's mind, it cleared out everything else. "I came to ask about baseball."

Reverend Robinette seemed to be having a bad time with the tie. He whipped that one out of his collar and threw it over on the bed, then tried another one, brighter colored this time.

Roy said, "I'm afraid I'm slipping into idolatry."

"Idolatry," said Reverend Robinette, staring hard in the mirror, as if he couldn't quite recall the meaning of the word. "Yes, sir, the team wears a graven image on their chests. They wear the head of a Greek soldier." Reverend Robinette grunted, and seemed to get what he wanted out of this tie. He turned and laid a hand on Roy's shoulder and stopped looking in the mirror. "Son," he said, "Do you make an idol of it?"

Roy meant to say No, no, it wasn't the insignia he meant, it was his teammates he was idolizing, but he couldn't find words quickly enough, so he said, "No, sir, I don't make an idol of that thing—"

"That's fine. That's what I expected to hear. You're a good Christian boy, Roy, and I know you try to witness for Jesus every day." He reached for his hairbrush. He seemed drawn irrevocably to his mirror.

Roy said, "That image don't mean a thing to me, but the team. I don't know if they're Christians. I know Coach is a Catholic—"

"In my father's house are many mansions, Roy," said Reverend Robinette, and Roy was puzzled because it wasn't a text they generally made a lot of at their church.

"But Reverend Robinette, I think sometimes lately I been playing for the team instead of for Jesus!"

Reverend Robinette thoughtfully looked over the rejected tie, then rolled it up and put it in his suitcase too. He snapped the suitcase shut. "Listen, Roy," he said, "I'm only a man. I can't see what's in your heart. And at this moment, I'm on my way to do very much an ordinary man's business. I only wish I was leaving this house a little neater, but I've never had much capacity for detail. And Roy, I know you came needing help, but I have to tell you that I need your prayers too. Will you pray for me?"

"Oh yes, sure, Reverend Robinette. But I have to ask you one more thing." Reverend Robinette had hoisted his suitcase. "I just need to know, does Jesus want me to play baseball?"

"You kneel right here and pray about it," answered Reverend Robinette. "You can use my Bible, and stay as long as you like. There's iced tea in the refrigerator, and milk—I think it hasn't gone sour yet. I meant to be on the road by now. This is the wrong day to be late, Roy. You relax here and pray. You talk to Jesus, and ask for yourself."

Roy knelt a long time beside Reverend Robinette's bed, which still had a few ties lying over it. He pressed his forehead into his fists and asked for a sign. He prayed so long, he got a little light-headed, and when he lifted his head, the first thing his eye fell on was the Bible on the nightstand. It was propped open with a half-eaten apple wrapped in a paper napkin. He couldn't take his eyes off the apple, and after a little while, it came to him that the apple was the sign he'd been asking for. The apple was a round thing like a baseball, and it was eaten up, ready to be discarded, and thus he had to discard baseball.

Thinking back now, Roy was bitter: that apple had been a sign all right, but it was a sign that Reverend Robinette had bit the apple, just like Adam the First Man. And like Adam, Reverend Robinette had been at that very moment on his way to be poisoned by a woman. And his poison had touched Roy, and made him quit playing baseball.

When school started, Roy went down to Viola to the consolidated high school. The very first day, he ran into two boys from the team. "Hey," they said. "Lookahere. It's the Ridge Runner, I guess the Ridge Runner is right glad we lost the tournament. I guess you like it like that, don't you, Ridge Runner?"

And the other boy said, "I don't call them hillbillies Ridge Runner, I call them Sheep Fuckers."

Roy knew he was being reviled and persecuted for His name's sake, he had even assumed that would happen, but he hadn't expected it to hurt, blows that went inside before they exploded. And he couldn't go talk to Reverend Robinette again, because of what had happened at the church.

Mrs. Robinette had moved in like a tornado with her piano, and then Wayne Wade began special prayer meetings a couple of nights a week in the September heat of the tractor barn. All the young people, except for Roy, stayed at the church, and kept on having their parties and their discussions and their ball games. The people who came with Wayne were the old ones, the ones who had been part of the church before Reverend Robinette. They brought their own lawn chairs to sit on; they complained about the games out in front of the church and the kissing out behind the church.

But Wayne wanted to talk about preaching. He wasn't satisfied with Reverend Robinette's speaking style. "He writes those sermons beforehand, I swear he does," said Wayne. "He don't wait for the spirit, he pre-pares those sermons." And, of course, there was the question of whether or not the new piano was of the devil, not to mention the fresh flowers Mrs. Robinette had been setting out on the pulpit every Sunday. And someone brought up whether anyone knew for sure Mrs. Robinette had been born-again, anyhow.

The night they brought that up was the night when Roy's mother, sitting with her arms crossed over her chest, snorted all of a sudden, "Well, if that woman ain't born-again, I don't know who is." And then added that, to tell the truth, *she* didn't see a thing wrong with a piano or flowers, you could praise the Lord just as well one way as the other, and all this secret meeting and talking was nothing but a lot of backbiting.

Roy's father's eyes got tiny and glittery, and Wayne Wade got down on his knees and asked Jesus whether or not they were backbiting, and before the night was over, they had voted in favor of separating from the Big Haul Church and having their own meeting here of a Sunday morning.

Then Roy and his mother and father walked silently up to the house and went in the kitchen, and Roy could see his father's eyes still glittering because a rule had been broken, and Roy's father lived by the rules. Roy began to feel tremendously thirsty and went to the refrigerator to get some milk.

His mother said, "I don't care, Preston. You and Roy can do what you want, but I don't intend to sit the rest of my life every Sunday morning and Wednesday night listening to Wayne Wade. I've *heard* Wayne Wade."

The funny thing was, Roy couldn't hear his father. He could hear his mother, and he could hear the glugging as the milk poured into his glass, and the glugging in his throat as he drank. He could hear it, but not feel it, but he could feel the hot pellets of words from his father, and not hear them.

His mother said, "I've been thinking maybe I'll just stop going to church for a while."

Roy's father stood up.

Roy's mother said, "I'm almost an old woman, Preston, and I'm tired of you running me like I was your mule."

That was what she shouldn't ought to have said: Roy's father believed where the Bible says the husband is the Head. That was an important text to Roy's father. Roy looked for his Bible to grab onto, but it was over near the telephone, so he had nothing to hold when his father smacked his mother backhand across the mouth, and Roy's hands started to shake and spilled the milk. He went for a rag, but his father said something and his mother said, "I'll get that later, Roy, you go on now."

Roy turned away with his hands still hanging in front of him. He hadn't seen this happen often, and he never thought about it between times, but when it happened, all the other times came back to him, one reflecting the other like they were caught in a hall of mirrors.

Roy went to bed, and lay down with his clothes on, holding his hands up in the air where he could watch them. He could still hear his mother's voice. Why doesn't she just shut up, wondered Roy, she knows what makes him mad. And then he started thinking maybe he was old enough now he should go in and tell her, or else ask his father to please stop.

But then the little Delilah ladies came drifting into his room and took his attention. Each one wearing a different color: ruby red, green, amethyst, all the diaphanous hues of the harem. The nearest one, green, floated right down between Roy's thighs, and he reached for his stones, but he'd forgotten to move them into the pockets of these pants, and his hands were right there, so he gave in to the little harlot.

The next day, Roy woke when he heard his father's truck leave. He still had his same clothes on, and he had to take them off and wash out his underdrawers. He put his pants back on with no undershorts and stuffed the wet undershorts under the pillow. When he finally went to the kitchen, he was like someone with a head cold, his brain vague and distant. His mother put a plate of eggs and bacon in front of him and fried slices of a late green tomato. He didn't look at her until she'd turned her back to him and was making the bologna sandwiches for his lunch. Her back looked okay, and her legs. But when she reached into the refrigerator, her arm showed, and he saw a big round mark, blue purple in the center, with red purple around the edge.

She sat down across from him. There was room at the table for a big family, but it was only full at Thanksgiving, when Roy's older brothers came home. His mother said, "I just want you to know, Roy, that if I ever hear of you doing some woman that way, I'll get off my deathbed if I have to and come and shoot you dead, even though you're my boy. You don't have to do that to be a man."

He didn't want to admit he understood her. He wished he could say in a deep voice, Let me eat in peace, woman. But he hadn't mastered that other way of talking, so he said, "Yes, ma'am. If I was to do that I hope you would shoot me."

"Well, I never would! I'd kill myself before I'd hurt you. I just mean ... Well, you know what I mean."

"Yes ma'am, I know."

"No you don't know. You don't know a thing." After a while,

she said, "Your eggs is getting cold." Still she didn't get up and finish making his lunch. "If he was a drunk," she said, "I might take it, because drunk is a sickness. But he ain't a drunk. And it just burns me for him to think he's got Jesus backing him up. Do you think Jesus if he'd of had a wife would of hit his wife? Do you think that, Roy?"

"Jesus never got married." This was an alarming idea to Roy. What if Jesus had come home with some woman like Mrs. Robinette? What if Jesus had met Delilah? Would nobody be saved now? "I know he never."

"I don't know if he did or he didn't," said his mother. "All any of us knows is what someone tells us. Oh, don't get big-eyed on me, Roy. I know we have the Bible, and I believe the Bible, what else do we have to go on, but the Bible says one thing here and one thing there, and Wayne and your Daddy pray and get one answer and Ellis and Mary Lou Robinette, they get a different answer, and I get something else again. But what I know for sure is I done things your dad's way a lot of years. Maybe some other day and age I might have to keep on taking it, and maybe if Aunt Emma didn't have her house in town."

Roy was still feeling this fuzziness, and he didn't quite follow about Aunt Emma's house.

"You know that old Pontiac Emma's got in her shed, Roy?" said his mother. "She wants me to learn to drive it. It ain't like I'm doing your father any good letting him beat on me, you know. You know that isn't a kindness to him or a help to his immortal soul." She sat for a minute longer and then said, "Well," and got up and finished her work in the kitchen, then went in the bedroom.

Roy ate, rinsed his plate, stacked it with the other breakfast things. Then he went out to wait for the school bus. His head felt even more like it had cotton stuck in the cracks once he was outside. It was still hot at the end of September. He sat down on the cement steps between the hydrangeas and realized he'd left his books and lunch inside. He didn't look back at the house, though. In front of him, down the dirt driveway, was the sheet-metal roof of the tractor barn and beyond it, the hill with the chunk stripped out of it, and beyond that, the tipple of the shaft mine just barely visible over the trees. All of a sudden, he could see it too clearly, and as if someone had pulled out all the cotton plugs, things started flowing out of him: coughs, sneezes, some tears, and here came the eggs and fried tomato. He just leaned over behind the hydrangea bush and let it pour out. I'm sick as a dog, he thought. He threw up like a dog, too, without any aftereffects, and he just went back to sitting. The bus pulled up and the driver leaned his elbow out the window and stared at Roy, and Roy stared back, and after half a minute, the bus drove off.

After another little bit, his mother came out in her blue nylon dress carrying the suitcase and her African violet. She said, "Well, I left things neatened up in the house."

"Yes, ma'am," said Roy.

"I was thinking you could come down after school today if you wanted to. I know Aunt Emma will say for you to come on and stay, if you want to. It would be convenient to school."

"I don't want to live at Aunt Emma's," said Roy.

"Well," said his mother, "you think it over. I'll be down there. You tell him."

I'm sick, Roy said in his mind, and it was so loud he didn't understand why she didn't hear it. It was almost like she just

ignored him. She walked with a lurch because of the weight of
the suitcase, and he saw her switch arms once, the suitcase to her
right hand, the violet to her left.

After she was out of sight, the little harem ladies came down
the hill, and it was the first time he saw them in daylight. Roy
whipped an imaginary twenty-two to his shoulder and picked
them off, one by one. Pee-ough! And the blue one drops over.
Pee-ough! There goes the red one, and Pow! That's all she wrote
for the one in green. The trouble was, they kept getting up, and
he had to shoot the same ones over and over.

That was how he knew about his rage. He knew about his
father's rage, and he knew about the wrath of God, but his
mother always said he was such a good-tempered boy.

After a while, he went inside and ate his bologna sandwich.

His dad came home at the usual time. Roy had been sitting
around all day, in the yard, on the porch. He was sitting on the
steps again when his dad pulled up. He watched his dad come
across the yard with his head down, his hair still wet from the
showers. He was little, dark, and bristly, with deep eyes. That's
how all the Critchfields looked, except Roy, and he was supposed
to be gangly and good-humored like his mother's family.

His dad hadn't seen Roy sitting there, and he gave a little jump.
"What're you doing home?"

Roy said, "I been waiting to tell you, she went to Emma's."

"Went down to Emma's, did she?" Roy followed him into the
house. "Did Emma take a spell?"

The dishcloth and the hand towel and the drying cloth were
all on the rack near the stove, dried stiff. On the windowsill was
a little water ring, but no African violet. Roy's father picked up

speed when he saw that, skipped the living room and went right into the big bedroom, where everything looked pretty ordinary except that the good chenille spread was on in place of the quilt. His father pulled open her sweater drawer, saw it was empty, and then opened her underwear drawer, and it was empty, too. He threw open the closet and stared at the empty half where her clothes should have been. He left everything open and started pacing around the room, cursing a blue streak.

He shouted some terrible names about her, and Roy couldn't hear them. He drew back his fist and punched Roy in the arm, and Roy felt the thud, but not the pain.

"Go on and hit me, Daddy," he said. He meant he was strong enough to take it, and his father should hit him instead of her, but his father's face was squeezed up like a baby's, tiny eyes, tiny mouth, little cheek balls, and he started making whimpering sounds and pulled out the underwear drawer and spun it across the room. It chunked into the wall and dropped to the floor, gouging the woodwork under the window.

They took the truck over to the body shop and picked up Wayne. When Wayne climbed in, he smacked Roy's knee. "We'll get your ma home," he said. "With the help of Jesus, we'll get her home in time for supper."

Roy's dad ground into a lower gear without benefit of a fully depressed clutch. He was still cursing.

Wayne said, "I know you're hurting bad, Preston. I been there myself, you remember. This thing ain't over till it's over, and you got the boy to think of and the Lord on your side."

Roy's dad shut up and actually avoided a hole in the road, and Roy felt gratitude to Wayne for his cheerful manliness. Wayne got born again when his wife left him, and that was also when he got so cheerful. Roy wondered if it was possible his own father would become more cheerful, too.

Roy's father said, "It ain't like she's some young girl."

"That's right," said Wayne. "She's a good woman, Preston, you know that. She's no fool."

"Then why'd she do this damn fool thing?" asked Roy's father.

They swung into the back street of town, then turned down the side street where Aunt Emma's house sat like an old farmhouse, its long porch at street level. The first thing they saw was the Robinette car parked out front. For half a second Roy imagined that Reverend Robinette must be inside and maybe everything would get worked out all at once: his parents, the two churches, maybe even Jesus and sports. But Mrs. Robinette came out wearing a white blouse and a bright yellow skirt.

"Shit-hole," said Roy's father. "Bitch from hell."

"Well, let's hear her out, Preston," said Wayne.

"We'll hear her, all right. Her mouth's been going like sixty before she ever got out the door."

She came right up to the truck and said, "Good evening, Wayne, Mr. Critchfield. Good evening, Roy."

"Good evening," said Wayne.

"I don't want to see you," said Roy's father. "I come to get Sis."

"Mrs. Critchfield asked me to say her aunt's not feeling well."

"That's too bad," said Wayne, showing his big smile teeth. "We're sorry to hear about Aunt Emma."

She said, "Mrs. Critchfield asked me to bring a message, and the message is, she doesn't want her aunt disturbed tonight. She'll be glad to talk tomorrow."

"Tomorrow!" Roy's dad pounded on the wheel with the heel of his hand.

"And she didn't ask me to tell you this, but I'm telling you for myself, and what I want to say is, Mrs. Critchfield needs a little recovery time, too. She needs a chance to heal up some *bruises*."

Wayne's eyelids fluttered, because he knew what *that* meant, but he said, "A man cleaves to his wife and they become as one."

Mrs. Robinette said, as quick as anything, "He's supposed to cleave *to* her, not cleave her in two." She jerked her head as she said this, and a little puff of flowers came through the window from her.

"Well," said Wayne, glancing around, "we just wanted to check and see she was settled in good. You know Mr. Critchfield is going to want to talk to her."

"And she wants to talk to him," said Mrs. Robinette. "But not tonight."

"Yes," said Wayne. "Well, we'll go on home."

Roy's father said, "Bitch! Goddam sonofabitch bitch."

When they were starting back up Big Haul again, Wayne said in his deep slow way, "We have a lot of praying and Bible studying to do tonight, Preston."

"Bitches!" shouted Roy's dad, hitting first the wheel with his hand, then swerving to hit a hole and then another one.

Wayne said, "Your father's hurting, Roy. He's in a lot of pain. But you just watch how Jesus can heal a man's heart."

Roy's father sucked air. "Yes," he said. "Yes, Jesus will. Jesus will put her back in my house."

"We hope and pray," said Wayne, "to see our way in this."

ROY AND HIS DAD had fried eggs and bacon every night that week because that was all Roy could cook. Sometimes, when Roy remembered, he would hunt for a green tomato in the garden, but they came out oily when he fried them. He attended school, and each day his teammates reviled him anew, and he would sit sweating through school, smelling his own armpits; sometimes the little harlots would float right in the air in ninth-grade math or civics class and set him swelling in his pants, and he'd almost cry from the raw burden of his body.

After school, he'd buy bread and bologna, and some kind of pie or cake, because he and his father both had a sweet tooth. Evenings, Wayne came over after supper with some of the church people to pray, so Roy didn't have all that much time to study. His father refused to go to town again to see his mother, in spite of all the praying and Bible reading. "I don't chew my cud twice," he said.

And then came this morning, when it seemed it couldn't stay hot one more day, but it did. Roy walked out of the house and realized he had forgotten his books again. He tried to turn himself around for his books, but it was like something was holding him in place. As if all the clouds piled up above and all the air that the science teachers insisted had weight was pressing down on him, nailing him to the ground, until his feet started pounding like they had some business of their own, and turned him around and marched him in the opposite direction of the school bus, through the berry bushes and over the hill, into the woods, then along the power company right-of-way.

Until he was standing on the strip mine road looking down at the Robinettes' house, clutching the stones in his pockets.

A little window in the house cranked open for ventilation, and he heard a miniaturized voice say "Honey—" and that was all it took for his rage to boil over. He ran down the hill, cocking back his arm as he ran, letting out a hyena yell. He took three great leaps and the stone went straight as a pine tree's shaft, and, even as the glass shattered, he cried out again and his left arm came up like a freight train, shattering another chunk of glass that had survived the first blast. Inside was a scream, and he came to a full stop, waiting for that scream to fill the air and carry him with it in an explosion, as emphatically—as finally—as when the bad guy's car goes over the cliff in the TV shows and bursts into flames.

But instead, there was a space of silence, the glass lying all over, blue cabinets and a yellow canister inside, then small whispers and movement.

Mrs. Robinette appeared first, carrying a broom in front of her and wearing a thin nightgown that made Roy dip his head in embarrassment. "Roy Critchfield?" she said.

Roy was confused. It was supposed to be over. He looked for something else to throw, and the nearest thing was a big pot of sprawling geraniums that he lifted, but the strength had gone out of him. He let it drop, and it fell on its side and the dirt spilled out.

"That's it," she said. "You stop right now, Roy." She called into the house, "Ellis! It's Roy Critchfield!"

Reverend Robinette came running out, and Roy had to look away from him, too, because his chest was bare except for its reddish curl of hair. He was wearing a towel. Naked as a Roman gladiator! thought Roy.

"What happened here?" Reverend Robinette seemed to say each word in a different tone: terror for "what," a deep frown around "happened," a puzzled "here."

Mrs. Robinette never took her eyes off Roy and never lowered her broom. "He broke the patio doors," she said.

Reverend Robinette waved his hand, as if this couldn't be.

"I did it," said Roy.

"We see who did it," said Mrs. Robinette. "We see that very well."

"Roy," said Reverend Robinette in his deep sad voice. It reminded Roy of how he had missed hearing it, especially hearing it read the Bible. "Oh, Roy."

Mrs. Robinette stepped out through the dangerous-looking slices of glass in slippers that left her feet bare at the arch and heel. "I'm not going to ask why you did this," she said, "because I think I know why. But I'm telling you now you're going to clean up every sliver of glass and pay for it, too. Do you hear me?"

He flinched, but took the broom she thrust at him. Then she squatted and began scooping the dirt back into the geranium pot. Roy could see the skin of her back through the nightgown, as diaphanous as anything the little harlots dared wear.

"Well, I don't know why," said Reverend Robinette. "Why did he break the glass?"

"Ask him," she said. "Roy, you start sweeping."

Reverend Robinette said, "Why, Roy?"

Roy tried to say something, but they were both looking at him. He swept. Reverend Robinette laid a hand on the broom. Roy said, "Because I'm like Samson, pulling it all down around my own ears."

Mrs. Robinette said, "Well, that may be, but we're not the Philistines. I'll call the glazier and find out how much it's going to cost to get this repaired."

"Now, Roy," said Reverend Robinette. "Tell me what this is about."

Roy could hear her on the phone in the kitchen, saying she had broken her patio doors with the broom, wasn't that a silly thing to do? He began to feel a twitching in his cheeks, around his eyes. He said, "I want to know what you meant about baseball. When I asked you that time about baseball, did you mean for me to quit it? Did you want me to stop?"

Reverend Robinette ran a hand through his hair. "I remember at the beginning of the summer you boys used to play some."

"You told me to pray about it. Don't you remember that day when I came over here?"

"On my wedding day? Well, Roy, you can't expect me to have said anything too sensible that day."

Roy was impressed with the thickness of the glass, how his stones, which he could see now were not all that big, must have been thrown very hard. Real scorchers, he thought. He said, "Well, I stopped playing after that. I gave it up, and now the boys at school revile me. They say foul things because I quit them."

She called out, "They say they can't give an estimate on fixing it until they come out and look, but he figures it has to be fifty dollars and maybe a lot more."

Reverend Robinette said, "There's been a misunderstanding, honey. Roy blames us for ..." he hesitated, "for interfering in his baseball career."

She disappeared and came back wearing a robe that matched

her nightgown, and he saw now that the towel Reverend Robinette was wearing was actually a little bath skirt with elastic and snaps. "I need a sack for the glass," said Roy. "How many hours do you reckon I'll have to work to make it up?"

"After school every day," she said. "For weeks and weeks."

Reverend Robinette got a brown grocery sack. "I suppose he could do some odd jobs at the church, too."

Roy was feeling unreasonably cheerful. "I'm not coming back to your church," he said. "I'll work off what I owe you, but you can't make me believe that 'make a joyful noise' means with a piano."

They looked at one another. Reverend Robinette said, "Your conscience is your affair, Roy, yours and Jesus's."

Again the unreasonable good cheer. Weeks and weeks of coming over here in the afternoons. Maybe they would invite him for dinner sometime, and there'd be mashed potatoes and some of the things he hadn't had since his mother left. They would talk about things and he would listen. They weren't really mad at him, he could tell. They were hoping to convince him to come back to their church. They would try to convince him to go visit his mother. He might have another talk with Reverend Robinette about baseball, too. Even Wayne Wade, who was so strict about everything else, said sports was good for a young man, kept his hands occupied.

Miracle of the
Locust Root

IN THE MOUNTAINS, we have a story about the time Jesus ripped up a locust tree that had been ruining an old man's garden; he told the root to take wing and fly home, and it did.

The lightness of the escaping root captivates us. So many of the stories of Jesus have a heavy quality, like daily life: The fishermen work all night and take nothing, so Jesus tells them to drop their nets one more time, and they haul up so many fish that the nets break. Simon becomes a disciple immediately, and Jesus tells him that now he will catch human beings as he once caught fish. It makes a nice simile. A solid, serviceable, impressive miracle; but heavy, like work shoes in a muddy field.

Likewise, his medical accomplishments: the lepers restored to health, the blind given back their vision. He made himself into everyone's fantasy of a competent, old-time doctor who never takes vacations. So what do we have today? Cataracts? Rub them with spittle. Scabies? Believe on me.

He recognized the problem himself. When Martha wanted help in the kitchen, Jesus told her that her sister, Mary, who wanted to skip the housework and get to the spiritual essence, had chosen the better part. You could tell he admired Mary. Martha was too much like him: What can I do for you? Loaves and fishes for five thousand? Something to mitigate the fear of death?

So, I love the story of the locust root. Jesus reaches his hand right through the crumbly soil and like magic pulls out a brown, hairy length of wood—this homely object that is wreaking everyday havoc in the garden of an old man with a trick knee who is trying to grow a little leaf lettuce and onions on the side of a mountain that is half slag anyhow and flooded every spring by the poisoned creek. Jesus just rips out this devil root and casts it away.

And in this miracle, the root doesn't end up in the trash heap either. No, Jesus goes the extra mile and gives the people what they want as well as what they need.

"And the root sprouts wings and does fly."

Just lifts off on wings of bark and resin, wings that last precisely as long as it takes to fly the root to its new home on the other side of the county. It drops a long way down and burrows into a hillside where the strippers didn't leave a single tree, and at once the eager progeny of the locust root sprout.

Someone in that barren place gives thanks for the hardy tree, and the old man with the garden gives thanks it is gone. And everyone—believer, unbeliever, disbeliever—swells with the palpable delight of gratitude.

Adventures of
the Vulture

Dear Mr. Hebert,

I have selected your establishment for the eventual disposition of my remains. I want you personally to prepare the obituary and deliver the eulogy. I am contracting for your services far in advance in order to make choices and arrange everything as I want: a brief memorial service in your funeral home with appropriate music, chosen by you; cremation; a notice in the paper that incorporates the biographical information I am about to give you, as should your talk. It is a simple life story, a few truths as I see them. I want my secrets exposed. The public will probably be disappointed by the lack of lust, blood, and incest, but expectations have been inflated under the influence of television.

My lifework has been to play the role of Viola's crazy lady who goes to funerals. You might begin my life story with something mildly risqué to capture their attention. The powder blue spring coat that I always wear to funerals belonged to my mother, as did the navy blue pillbox hat with the veil. My mother would wince to know that I wear navy and powder blue together, but

Viola will find far more interesting that the coat often covered a sweatshirt and rolled up pedal pushers or, in hot weather, a pair of baby doll pajamas. Yes, Mr. Hebert, and if you find the idea of a woman of my years wearing baby doll pajamas too vulgar to mention, then I will be forced to go to another funeral parlor, although Hebert's has been my first choice from the day I arrived in Viola.

I have always loved your polished marble and granite. As far as I have been able to discern, there is no plastic on the premises, although I presume you use those little plastic blocks to shore up the sinking cheeks of the deceased. Even you, Mr. Hebert, have a high gloss to your nails, a naturally waxy complexion, and such a fine head of hair! You yourself are the most superlative of your fixtures with your vibrant, yet serene, baritone. Without being unctuous, you are more reassuring than any of the preachers in Viola. You can make the most disturbing, heartrending, or even grotesque statement, and your audience feels uplifted. You still the waters, Mr. Hebert.

I have never forgotten the time when the deceased's divorced husband showed up at the funeral and the surviving husband started to curse and then moved as if to attack the other. You, Mr. Hebert, never hesitated: in spite of your weight, your age, and the crisp creases in your suit, you put your body between the two men and miraculously convinced the enraged bereaved that what he thought was an affront was actually a compliment to the good character of his wife. And both husbands stayed. You have a power, Mr. Hebert. I have thought about this a long time, and my conclusion is that we trust you because you are no hypocrite. You only promise what you can deliver: a well-organized funeral, high quality makeup, satin pillows that coordinate with casket linings. I would have an affair with you in a minute, Mr. Hebert, if you were game. I have a fantasy of lying in one of your biers, and you coming to me ever so quietly, still wearing your dark gray suit.

My first secret, Mr. Hebert, is that I am a skeptic vis-a-vis the supernatural, and you know how seriously we take our religious affiliations here in the mountains. Perhaps that is your secret, too? I am not asking, of course; but I speculate. Or is your secret something more exquisitely shocking? Do you have intimacies with your corpses? Or is it only that you pick your nose or eat chocolates during embalming? I know you have secrets; we keep our souls in little private pouches, Mr. Hebert. You must be a materialist, sub rosa, at least. How else could you make a living by preserving what should rightly return to the earthworms?

I grew up just over the ridge in Moorestown, so I came to Viola knowing your ways. I know how every town has its atheist as well as its funeral lady. Our Moorestown atheist was a gentleman named Dower Brown, although I think in retrospect he was less an atheist and more an exhibitionist. Dower used to corner the ministers over their morning coffee at AJ's Restaurant to challenge them on the virgin birth or the extent of Noah's flood. He used to show up at prayer meetings at our church and cry, "But tell me, why are there no more miracles? God knew all those multiplied loaves and fishes would be hearsay by the time it got to us. If God works by miracles, why not give us miracles now? Let Him step down and disarm the nuclear missiles. Let Him give us so much oil we'll never be dependent on the Arabs again! Where are the miracles today?"

I believe most people secretly have some sympathy for Dower's position. Who doesn't hunger for the concrete? Even my mother said once, on the way home, "It would be nice to have a miracle in Moorestown, wouldn't it?"

But Dower was too passionate; he wanted God to overcome him, and apparently God did, because I heard shortly before I left that he was studying with the priest at St. Ann's. I, on the other hand, have never opposed God. I simply have a bone-deep intuition that this flesh, the messages darting along these synapses— that these are as far as it goes. That all the promises of the Golden Shore have been misinterpreted. Is there a God? Perhaps. Did He take Mother to join Daddy in First Baptist of Moorestown, West Virginia Heaven? I doubt it. I visit your Chapel of the Bereaved, Mr. Hebert. I gaze at your corpses, with their hair set and their pancake makeup. I sign the guest book, then go back again to contemplate the nails and eyelids, and I know I am looking at a finished thing.

My second secret is that I was disappointed at how long my mother lasted. I was the youngest of three daughters, and the others had long since left home when my mother got sick. The fact that I was the one to stay with her was a happenstance, not a choice, and I think I resented this most of all. Not the constrictions I lived under—which were not so much worse than the ones I live under now—but how my life happened to me with no conscious choosing. Did you consider pharmacy and dentistry before you settled on mortuary, Mr. Hebert? I hope so. My job at

Garner's Dress Shop was a summer makeshift—what I happened to be doing while I decided whether to use my college graduation money to sail directly to Europe or to spend some months in New York first. I stayed home that summer because my father had died over the winter, and Mother was lonely. Then they found the lump in her breast, and she had her operation, and I stayed for twenty-five years. I wasted my youth planning my escape.

That was the summer of 1955, and we figured she had a year to live, perhaps two. I sometimes think she lived so long because she knew I'd never keep her house the way she liked it. It was brand-new—they'd moved into it only four months before Daddy's heart attack. It was what they had always wanted: a house with no ancient dirt between the floorboards, with no wallpaper under the wallpaper. They thirsted for factory-new Early American "antiques" and low-maintenance vinyl siding, for tilt-in windows. They both came from coal mining camps, you see, so it was their affliction to worship the new and the clean. Your Viola is a more diversified town economically than Moorestown, which had only the mines. Everyone there grew up with coal dust in their ears, and my mother spent her energies in keeping scratches off her cherry wood hutch and weeding her borders of impatiens. Pale pink impatiens, of course, because bright colors repelled her. She recoiled especially from anything yellow or red, which she associated with the immigrant girls who used to live on the bottom street in her company town. To my mother, bright colors, loud frying, and possibly even hearty laughter were the signs of a lower social station.

My third secret is that I loved all those things: theatrical gestures, the color red, anything packed in olive oil, and John DeMarco. John was my lover for most of the years I stayed in Moorestown. Oh, my solid, square John. A big eater and laugher, with twinkles in the corners of his eyes. Older than I, married with children—a Catholic, of course—and my father's employee. Many times forbidden to me. You need not allude to him by name, Mr. Hebert, but I would like it to be known that I had a lover. And do mention that I loved bright colors and olive oil. At least it will explain the cases of imported artichoke hearts in my pantry.

MY MOTHER DIED at long last unexpectedly of a stroke, perhaps related to her various cancers and perhaps not. She collapsed on her new aluminum walker in the backyard, never releasing her trowel. In a panic of shock and guilt and relief, I made bad choices about the funeral. Our minister was out of town and the substitute I picked got her name wrong. Isn't that a horror? A faithful church lady all her life, and the stupid idiot called her Ida instead of Edna. He did not once touch on her real life's work, which was the conservation and improvement of that impeccable house. I confess I overreacted, speaking out loud and thrashing about in the church pew.

My sisters were concerned about me, and I think they were right, because I had a kind of breakdown. I locked myself in the downstairs bathroom, where I kept my secret supply of Oliverio's Italian peppers, and I ate an entire pint with my fingers, leaning against the sink.

My sisters knew something was wrong. You'll be so lonely in that house! they said, meaning, What crazy thing are you going to do when we leave? I didn't brush my hair, I paced, I ate hot peppers—and no longer secretly, but in front of them. While my sisters were drinking coffee in the kitchen with the boxes of insurance forms, I slipped out to the pay phone at the Dairy Mart and got information on setting up bank accounts in other cities. I inquired of realtors about selling the house and its contents by proxy. I was having a breakdown, but a cagey, shrewd one. My sisters finally left, and I assigned rights and filed affidavits. I composed letters telling each of them I was cutting my ties. I wrote John DeMarco that I was going to ride the Orient Express and then take a cruise around the world. He shouldn't try to contact me, perhaps I'd send postcards. Perhaps not.

In the dead of night, not having slept in three days, I packed the Chevelle and drove north and east, taking the small roads, stopping for an hour to watch the sun rise over the Allegheny Front. I bought half a bushel of apples in Maryland and ate them at scenic overlooks, I chatted with retired people on a bus trip and made up lies about where I was going.

As afternoon wore on, I knew I was in a strange mental state, but I pretended it was just fatigue. I made frequent stops to drink coffee. I bought a pack of cigarettes and smoked them one after another, until I was nauseated. It was night again when I reached the New Jersey Turnpike. I had developed a sinus headache that I blamed on cigarettes and the refineries.

I had cash and credit cards. Why didn't I find a motel until my headache was gone? Why didn't I find a place with a shower and a firm mattress, sleep as long as I wanted, get a good breakfast, and sit back to think about the past and the future? But I guess I wanted to be lost. I craved my crisis.

Instead, cars passed me, honking, trucks exploded on two sides. My vision blurred with the headache, and I moved over to the service lane, and drove there mile after mile. I remember the throbbing of pain, but not how I guided the car. I saw thin, ghostly towers ahead and thought they were New York. I remember half-ducking from sudden large green presences that turned out to be exit signs for Staten Island and the Holland Tunnel. I kept driving across exiting traffic, and each time there were screaming horns. Someone should have locked me up for the night. They would have, too, in a small town, wouldn't they, Mr. Hebert? In Moorestown or Viola they would never have let me endanger myself and others like that.

I found another rest stop and laid my forehead on the steering wheel. The pressure seemed to equalize the pressure inside my head, and I lifted myself enough to look at my arm, at the flesh over my wrist, where there were some silvery hairs picking up light from the high sodium lamps, and I became convinced that my body hair had turned white, that I had plunged into old age without knowing it. I stumbled inside and found in the bathroom mirror that I still had some brown hair, that my cheeks had not sunken.

The rest stop was one of those ugly plastic caverns in all the colors that alarmed my mother. I know the people were not as terribly distant from one another as they appeared to be. I know they must have been coming out of the bathrooms, looking at maps, making phone calls, doing all the things they usually do in those places, but they seemed to me to be floating underwater, corpses caught in the seaweed, so far away. I sat down.

A couple of tables away was one man who seemed alive. I remember he was chewing, and wearing a cap that said BUDWEISER. But mostly, Mr. Hebert, I was drawn to him because he had the same reassuring chunky build as John DeMarco.

I called out, "You remind me of John DeMarco from Moorestown, West Virginia."

He nodded his head, more or less politely. I don't suppose he really heard me. I stumbled over the five steps to join him at his table, and I could suddenly see very clearly, but only him: the five o'clock shadow, the kind of lips that are always moist. Joining him at that table was not the kind of behavior they taught me in Moorestown, Mr. Hebert. This part is hard to relate. I have relived it a hundred thousand times and still don't understand myself.

I said to this stranger, "I seem to have run out of steam. Did that ever happen to you? Did you ever run out of steam? You're not related to John DeMarco are you? Are you Italian? Of Italian descent?"

The man said, "Listen, lady, I don't mean to be rude, but what business is that of yours?" He sounded like he was from up there, New York or New Jersey.

I believe I started talking about appliances. I believe I told him how John really liked repairs, not selling. How he always closed the shop early so he could go in the back and fix, but how he did it in his suit. How I used to join him back there. It was my father's shop first, you know. I used to love to watch John's wrists when he was working. I think I talked at great length about John DeMarco to this stranger drinking coffee and chewing cheeseburger. When had I ever had anyone to talk to, Mr. Hebert? Might I have stayed in Moorestown if I'd had someone to talk to?

I remember, even as I talked, wondering what kind of hair this man had under his cap, if it was the dense wavy kind like John's. I believe I asked him to take off his hat.

"I think you better go about your business, lady," he said.

I believe I told him my theory that baldness indicates extreme masculinity because only men are bald.

He glared from under the bill of his cap and said, "Listen, I'm a family man."

It occurred to me then that he thought I was making a pass at him. I was wearing old pedal pushers and ankle socks, and a blouse that overhung my bosom as if I had twice as much belly. I was flattered to be mistaken for something so well-defined, and instead of disabusing him—you will not approve of this, Mr. Hebert, but remember my state of mind—I said, "Oh my goodness, you think I'm—well, who knows, perhaps I am." It was like playacting. I wracked my brains for what one of those women would say. I said, "Hey, do you want to party? I guess I know how to give a man a good time. I'm not the freshest, you know, but very cheap. I've been on the road for eighteen hours or more. No sleep, no toothbrush. But very cheap."

"Listen," he said, "I'm stuck here all night because I'll be damned if I'm going to drive into New York City in the middle of the night, and I want to be left alone. I mean it. I want to be left alone."

I think I asked him again if he were Italian-American.

"None of my business is none of your business," he said. "Do you get my meaning?"

I said, "I don't really care about your roots. Or rather, I want to know about your hair roots. I just want to know if you're bald."

He firmed the bill on his hat and got up. I got up too. He said, "I don't need this tonight. I don't need any crazy ladies. I have a headache."

Was that the moment I received my calling, Mr. Hebert? When he called me a crazy lady? I know I felt some kind of rush of hope. I said, "I have a headache too! And that's the truth, although I have to confess I was lying about being a lady of the night."

He started to walk away. I didn't want to be left alone. I believe I lunged at his hat.

I must have lunged, because I distinctly remember that he blocked, gave me a solid push in the shoulders.

I thank him for that, Mr. Hebert. The room settled, shrank down to normal size, and I heard a sort of normal thought in my head. I believe I told myself, This is crazy. But I came at him again anyhow, and again he shoved me away, harder this time. I lost my footing on a wet patch of floor, skittered, but stayed upright. I was like one of those country boys who comes into town and gets drunk, and yearns to feel a fist, to feel. I moved forward, and he backed into the coatrack. For an instant, we both hesitated, and there was a multitude of possibilities: he could have broken my jaw, I could have shrugged and walked away.

I said, "I just want to see your hair."

He whipped off the hat and spun it into my face. It struck me across the bridge of the nose hard enough to make my eyes tear. I turned away to follow the hat, stooped to pick it up. By the time I turned back again, he was out the door, and I never got to see his hair after all. I ran out too, carrying the hat. I went from truck to truck, but I never found him. Finally, I put on the Budweiser cap and started home.

I had lied. I wasn't a prostitute, of course, but if he had been willing to make love in the cab of his truck, I probably would have done it gladly. I would have done anything to ease my aching.

THE REST OF IT will not make you uncomfortable, Mr. Hebert.

There were stars over Pennsylvania, but fog in Maryland. I crawled up and down the mountains, barely able to see, but then, towards morning, there were stars again over West Virginia. I could see swooping ridges by starlight, and how they gradually gathered into the familiar humpy hills. I parked on the shoulder for a while, climbed up on the hood of my station wagon and lay back, feeling the warmth of the engine under me, smelling the black night wetness, and I made up an idea, a sort of practical joke. I would come back to some town like Moorestown but not Moorestown, and I would pretend I was returning after many years' absence. I would pretend I had left to go away to college and was only now returning. I would ask after nonexistent friends and relatives and wonder what happened to them. I would tell startling adventures from my life. I would tell them I lived with a sculptor in Greenwich Village during the Beatnik years and rode the Orient Express across Afghanistan and participated in a revolution. That I lived in a palazzo in Venice, on the Left Bank in Paris. I fell asleep until the engine began to cool and a damp dawn wind lapped over me. A rainy fog enveloped everything; I drove on. With a feeling that I was finally on the right path, I passed the exit for Moorestown and got off at Viola. I first had in mind to visit various towns until I found the right one for my project, but as I drove the fifteen slow miles from the interstate into Viola, I felt the sensation of settling again.

Viola, like Moorestown, has a railroad and a river. Like us, you are not quite near enough the interstate for easy off-and-on. But, unlike Moorestown, you had your rich Mr. Hodgkiss who gave you some public buildings. I stopped in the parking lot behind the Methodist church. Yes, Mr. Hebert, by coincidence, also the parking lot for Hebert's Funeral Home.

I took another nap, and when I woke up, I looked around pretty thoroughly, at my leisure, examining everything I could see without getting out of the car. I had this odd sensation of one view superimposed over another. I was seeing Viola and Moorestown both at once, and the little variations were like looking through a stereopticon—the slightly different angles give you depth of vision, or at least the illusion of depth. I dug down in the pocket of my pedal pushers and found a Drake's coffee cake and ate it until the drizzle started. Then I noticed people arriving at the church: the limousine, the hearse. I didn't have a raincoat, but mother's spring coat was in a paper bag in the back, so I wore that. It was a small funeral, for an elderly gentleman I never heard anyone mention again from that day to this. I enjoyed the singing as I always do, and I thought the minister's remarks were extremely well-taken. "He was the kind of man who gave nickels to little boys for ice cream," the minister said. "He gave nickels to little boys long after an ice cream cone cost half a dollar, and do you know what? He was the kind of man that the little boys never told him any different." I found myself crying over this old gentleman I'd never known, and I cried all the way through the rest of the service.

AFTERWARDS, I VISITED HEBERT'S and signed the guest book for whomever your corpse was that day. I think you had a couple of them, I don't really remember. I found a newspaper, I got my room at Mrs. Critchfield's house. The room has its own toilet, sink, and kitchen, though you have to share the tub with Mrs. Critchfield. But it works out fine because she and I neither one want to dry out our skin with over-many baths. Later, I went to the grocery store and bought things to stock my cabinet. I bought things that I used to keep under the sink in the bathroom or in the trunk of the car: my packaged cakes from Hostess and Drake; lots of canned fish in oil, like sardines and anchovies; anchovy paste, too; and herring in mustard sauce; my artichoke hearts, of course; and several kinds of olives and hot peppers. I put up open shelves for storing my groceries, and I set them out in plain view. They please me, Mr. Hebert, to look at and to eat.

This is my retirement home. I don't worry about my figure or my breath. And you'd be surprised by the number of men who ask me out anyhow.

Late at night I read stacks of library books and listen to the radio talk shows in bed with hot peppers and ginger snaps. Sometimes I stay home till I run out of canned goods. I let the oily old cans and jars pile up on the floor and table. I don't change out of my nightgown. It seems like sacrilege to speak of such slovenliness to you, Mr. Hebert, with your fingernails that are cleaner than most people's silverware.

But you needn't take me too seriously, I'm just the crazy funeral lady. All I ask is for you, or your heirs—should I outlive you, to take charge of my funeral arrangements. And you must agree by now that the obituary will not be a huge shocker, except perhaps for the headline, in which I want you to refer to me by the name the children call me. Back in Moorestown we used to call our funeral lady Hannah Hearse. I want my headline to read, THE VULTURE PASSES.

What I am trying to do, of course, is nail down my life as best I can, the way you can nail down a coffin. I am making my choices well in advance. I enclose a check as a retainer. I want everything as regular as a Hebert's Funeral Home funeral can be.

And here's a funny thing: Over the last few years, as I've been making these decisions, I have found that there is something else I want. Perhaps I've attended enough funerals for now. I find myself thinking that I might take a trip after all. I might contact my sisters and go for a visit, or even go back to Moorestown and see if John DeMarco is still living. I might on the other hand just sign up for one of those senior citizen bus trips, or call a travel agent.

The last thing I'll need from you, Mr. Hebert, is a separate estimate for transporting a body, should I die en route, back from Moorestown or New York or Europe, or perhaps even the Far East. Wherever I end up, I want to rest assured I will still have my Hebert's Funeral Home funeral.

Sincerely,
The Funeral Lady

To Speak Well
of the Dead

I couldn't get over the feeling that Brad Aikens's funeral was a picnic. We had borrowed a car; we had chicken and sprout sandwiches on whole wheat and two liters of Diet Pepsi. We were cutting classes, and I had Barbara to myself. She was more somber than I, in her dark suit, her thick, wild hair knotted at the nape of her neck—but Brad had been her friend more than mine, although she'd stopped seeing him, too, just like everyone else. He'd spent his last days in public places, drinking, smoking, and sniffing in total defiance of all university and town regulations. He killed himself by jumping off a fire escape; a couple of students leaving a bar found him at least six, maybe twelve hours later. Barbara said she couldn't stop imagining the details.

We drove south on the interstate that morning through mountains dun-colored with the muddy trunks of trees. I said, "Maybe Brad's problem was that he started to fade out. I can't remember what he looked like. I mean, it's like he was transparent: nobody noticed, no matter what outrageous thing he did."

Barbara turned her face away from the steering wheel for a

second, and I saw that she hadn't worn lipstick, but she was wearing more eye makeup than usual. "This may be profound," she said, and I warmed at the compliment.

Barbara was from Queens, New York, and she kept saying she couldn't believe she was going to college in Appalachia. She said we should transfer out, the two of us together, and be roommates somewhere else. When I mentioned this idea to my parents, they began mailing me articles clipped from *USA Today* about urban crime. Brad's hometown was Viola, just up the river from my town. We used to play them in football. "It amazes me," I told Barbara, "that a person like Brad could come from a town like Viola."

Barbara changed lanes to avoid a semi that was crawling up the hill, and as she did, something slid out from under the seat and picked my stocking. I reached down and pulled up a hiking boot with two inch soles and a fuzzy plaid liner.

She said, "If the car breaks down, I don't want to have to hike out of here in high-heeled pumps."

"We aren't going to the Arctic tundra, Barbara. There'll be phone booths and maybe even gas stations and grocery stores. I heard they were getting a Pizza Hut in the Interior, too."

She called everything the Interior, except the university, where at least, said Barbara, you could find the odd chamber concert, although the emphasis should be on the *odd*. Sometimes she would stare for a long time and then exclaim how amazing it was that a person like me could come from a place like this, and sometimes I was deeply flattered, and sometimes—or even at the same time—I wanted to slap her face.

I told her when to get off the interstate, navigating without a map. The last few miles to Viola were through farmland and woods.

"Lookit—" she said suddenly, "did you see all those crosses?"

There were three of them: two blue, and one orange, or maybe it was meant to be gold. They were ten or twelve feet high, sitting in the middle of a field with some black Angus steers moseying around their bases. "It's the crucifixion," I said.

"I figured that out. But why are there three of them?"

"The one in the middle is for Jesus, and the others are the two thieves."

"What thieves?"

"The thieves who got crucified with him. The one who went to heaven and the one who didn't."

"*Three* crosses? I never knew there were *three* crosses. How come they've got them on that farm?"

"There's this guy who puts them up. He has an idea to put them coast to coast, so you're never out of sight of them."

Barbara started to frown. "Isn't it illegal to put religious symbols up in public places? There was this thing about nativity scenes in some town in New England."

"I suppose he gets permission from the farmer. The farmer can put whatever he wants in his own field, I guess."

"But everyone has to look at it. It's like an establishment of religion."

I shrugged. "It seems sort of tacky."

"Tacky!" said Barbara. "I'd say it's worse than tacky. I'd say it's shoving your religion down other people's throats."

"Nobody complains. Not here—everyone's some kind of Christian here."

"Great. Thanks a lot. I feel real welcome. Maybe I'll just send them my name and address in case they need a lawn to burn a cross on." She hit the brakes and swerved onto the shoulder, which was very narrow at that point, and almost dropped us into a ditch. The engine died, and I found myself gazing at a length of barbed wire.

I tried to speak quietly. "Barbara, it's just one guy—"

"There's never just one guy. They always have an organization. I bet it's the Klan or the Aryan Nation or something. If they knew I was Jewish, they'd probably string me up. On one of the crosses."

"Barbara!"

"I mean it! I'm not joking."

"They just—I don't know—they believe in trying to convince other people to believe what they do."

"Right, it's called a pogrom. Where are those cigarettes?" We had found a pack in the glove box of the borrowed car. "And don't say anything to me about smoking, I know they aren't good for you."

"Maybe I'll have one too."

"Not you." She snatched the pack away and shoved it into the pocket on the car door without taking one herself. "I don't want to be responsible for you getting cancer in twenty years."

We were very health conscious, rejecting red meat in the cafeteria, peeling our fruit. We had talked at some length about whether to bring the no-caffeine or regular Diet Pepsi. She sighed. "Are they going to shove a lot of religion down my throat at this funeral? Are they going to say how Brad is having a big party up in heaven? I couldn't take that, because Brad's got a lot to do with hell and not much with heaven."

"Methodists are generally pretty calm these days."

"They'd better be. I don't want to see crosses everywhere."

"It's a church, Barbara."

"Oh, you know what I mean. This whole thing is spacing me. Why didn't they just stuff him in the ground? Or cremate him? Why do they have funerals anyhow?"

"It finishes things off. It makes it all seem connected. I don't know. You're the one who insisted on coming."

"I've never been to a funeral before, you know."

"You were never at a funeral? I thought you said it was so important to go to a funeral if someone you know dies."

"It is important, but my parents always sent me to someone's house to play. And recently, nobody in my family died, except my uncle, and my parents didn't tell me until the funeral was over. If they hadn't been so afraid of traumatizing me, I wouldn't be so traumatized."

BY THE TIME we found the church, parked, squared our shoulders and slipped into a back pew, the minister was already talking about a young boy who used to do chores for widows. He walked their dogs, said the pastor, cut their grass, and never took a penny, just acted out of his fine good nature.

I glanced at Barbara to see how she was taking it. I supposed what he said could be true. Barbara was looking up at the ceiling, which was painted peach between dark rafters. Down front there were spears of gladiolus and the polished oak of the closed casket. I couldn't remember anything unkind about Brad. When he got crazy, he didn't torture cats or molest little girls. I could picture him with a dog, part hound, who leaped and yipped in happiness to be going out-of-doors. I had a rush of nostalgia for the life Brad had given up: the dog, the opportunity to go to funerals.

It had been a long time since I'd sat comfortably in a church with my mind drifting; I'd stopped going to church my junior year in high school. The minister ended now, before I was ready. They sang, "Blessed Be the Tie that Binds," and men in dark suits carried the casket up the aisle.

Barbara grabbed my arm. "He's in that box, isn't he?"

"What did you think was in the casket? At the funeral home you would have had to look at the corpse. And up in the hollows they preach over an open casket—"

"Stop. I don't want to think about it."

Before leaving, most of the people were going over to a woman under the windows on the far side. Backlighting from the colored glass windows made it hard to see her face. A large teenage boy stood beside her, younger than Brad, softer contoured, hair brown rather than blond, but unmistakably his brother.

I said, "I suppose we should go pay our respects."

"Is that what you do?"

"Well, it's what everyone else is doing." We hung back a little, but soon there were no more shoulders between us and the shaded woman, so I said, "We're friends of Brad's, from the university."

"From the university!" The woman didn't quite clap her hands, but reached out as if to embrace us, then didn't complete the gesture. "You came so far!" she cried. "It's Brad's college friends, Billy. It's friends of Brad's from the university." She introduced us to a man her own age, her brother, then to an elderly great-uncle who had stunning white hair and didn't seem to hear well. As far as I could see, there was no father for Brad and Billy. "Some of Brad's college friends!" she kept saying. "All the way from the university!"

She asked us to drive in the cortege to the Masonic cemetery, then back to the house for something to eat. I was glad, because I hadn't gotten enough funeral. There was something in all this I had been missing. Magisterial in my superior knowledge, I told Barbara, "Put your lights on. Leave a space between you and the next car."

"How did we get so close to the front? I can't be in the front."

"You won't be. We wait for the hearse and the car with the family in it to lead us."

It was a perfect day, I thought. Austere. Domination of earth colors. The sun came out, dried grass and mud took on tones of yellow and rust, and the tips of the twigs were purple. A faint odor of dirt came from the pile beside the grave, the call of a crow, the dark nuggets of words dropped by the minister, the silence surrounding Brad's mother and brother. This is, I kept thinking. *This is.* Then the creak of the ropes.

"There," said Barbara, when the casket was down. "That's done."

THE AIKENS HOUSE bustled with women who had gone directly from church to set out food. Even with the women, though, the house had a spare quality. The pictures on the wall were widely separated, the furniture aligned with the straight edges of the rug.

"It looks just like home," I said, trying to joke, but Barbara had lowered her head to give people one of her intense stares.

A broad-smiled woman with gray wings in her hair introduced herself as Aunt Martha, although she wasn't really their aunt, she said. She pressed plates into our hands and gave us a tour of the buffet table, pointing out sliced ham, Jello-and-Cool-Whip fruit salad, homemade Irish soda bread, and double chocolate brownies.

She watched us fill our plates. "We all appreciate how far you came," she said. "It means so much to Phyllis." I wanted to spear the biggest fried chicken breast, but Aunt Martha kept watching, so I took a more modest drumstick instead. Aunt Martha said, "A lot of us were saying how pleased we were—to know Brad had friends at the university. He didn't seem to be doing all that well the last few months."

"He had basically dropped out," said Barbara. She would have explained more fully, but they called Martha for a problem with the coffee urn extension cord. Barbara said, "They're all dying to know which one of us slept with him. That's what they really want to know."

"Oh, I don't think so." I was probably being naive, or maybe just more interested in the sweet fruit salad I hadn't meant to take because there wasn't a thing nourishing in it, except maybe the tiny mandarin orange slices. Somehow it seemed the right thing to eat here. Funeral meats and sickening sweets.

The problem with the coffee urn solved, it looked like Aunt Martha was about to come back, but Brad's mother herself walked in the front door. She passed her heavy coat to her brother, but wouldn't give up her black velvet beret, which made her head seem too heavy for her thin neck. Her black dress was for summer, with cap sleeves that bared her upper arms. The arms seemed soft, and her stomach, too. Something slack about her, vaguely embarrassing. She glanced at us as Martha tried to give her coffee.

Barbara nudged me. "She spotted us."

People kept talking to her, but she moved steadily across the room toward us. We backed off, until we were stopped by the wall under a display of three china plates in an eighteenth century hayrick design.

Brad's mother's head bobbed under the beret. "All the way from the university," she said, and stumbled, turned over on her ankle, and had to catch herself on Barbara's arm. "I'm fine," she said. "I'm really okay. You'd think I never wore high heels before." She laughed out a tiny burst of noise.

Barbara leaned her face very close to Brad's mother. "Mrs. Aikens," she said, "I wasn't sure I wanted to say this, but I think I need to tell you. It was partly my fault about Brad."

Mrs. Aikens gave Barbara's forearm a quick pat. "It's so good to know he had good friends."

"But the point is," said Barbara, forehead practically touching Mrs. Aikens's now, "the point is, all his friends failed him. None of us were there when it all hit the fan. Do you understand? No one was *there* for him?"

"Oh no," said Mrs. Aikens. "I'm sure you didn't fail anyone."

"I *did* fail him. I could see he was falling apart. I mean, he was coming undone at the seams—"

"Seams?" murmured Mrs. Aikens, the smile fading, rolling her eyes toward the hayrick on the mounted plate. "His clothes?"

Impatient, as she often was when she thought someone was being willfully dense, Barbara said, "No, no, of course not his clothes. It was his *personality*. It was a total failure of all systems."

Mrs. Aikens teetered a little, hugged her own arms. "Why, you couldn't see the future, honey. How could you have known he was going to slip and fall off that fire escape? What could you have done?"

"My God," said Barbara, looking at me. "She doesn't know."

Aunt Martha had not been far away. "You haven't had a bite to eat yet, Phyllis."

"Not now," said Barbara. "I have to explain something to her. She doesn't understand—"

Martha used her smile broadside on Barbara, and simultaneously blocked with her hip, herding Brad's mother away. "I don't think Phyllis needs to talk right now," she said. "She needs to eat."

"I think I just might have a bite," said Brad's mother, smiling far off beyond the hayrick now. "It was so good of you girls to come."

I couldn't help myself from murmuring, "All the way from the university."

"Oh yes," smiled Mrs. Aikens, "from the university."

"She's on downers," Barbara said. "She thinks Brad is on the heavenly campus greensward. How can she not know he killed himself?"

"She knows," I said.

"Then why would she lie? How could you lie about your son's suicide?"

"She knows, but she isn't admitting the truth to herself."

"That isn't knowing, that's lying to yourself." Barbara's hair shifted ominously on her neck as if it were about to come free of its pins and all hell break loose.

I said, "Don't you see? They all know. Why else would Aunt Martha be so protective and get her away from us? They know, but that doesn't mean they're going to say it out loud, not to each other, not to themselves."

"In other words, they don't want to hear that Brad was hurting so bad he killed himself."

'That's right. They don't want to hear it. They don't want to hear it in so many words. They don't want to hear it in words at all."

"Well, I'm sorry, but I can't accept that. This is the one thing in his life Brad ever said loud and clear. He was murky a lot of the time, but he wanted people to hear this."

"How do you know?" And why was I taking this position? I felt as if I was down in the herd with the friends and neighbors, while Barbara was on the mountain, the one with the leonine head and the Word. But I persisted: "I mean it, How can you be so sure? How do we know he really did it on purpose anyhow? Maybe he slipped or was pushed, we weren't there. I can't even remember what he looked like. Maybe he wished all along just to be normal, you know, do what the rest of us were doing at college, or maybe he wanted to come back down here—"

Barbara's eyes grew enormous, and there were little flecks of gold in her irises. "Focus on the pain," she said. "*His* pain."

I was slipping under her spell, although I didn't really believe she was right. I didn't believe what she said, but I didn't believe what I was saying either. "Barbara, these people aren't as good at being explicit as you are. Even Brad—you know—he didn't say it in words."

"Then I'll have to put it in words for him. He deserves that much." She touched my arm. "It's okay," she said. "They can take it." She took a few steps to the couch where Mrs. Aikens's uncle was sitting with his wavy white hair. Barbara's hair was uncoiling down her back, beginning to unspring. "Brad killed himself," she said gently. "I know it's hard, but I think you need to face it."

The great-uncle struggled to his feet and shook Barbara's hand. "Pleased to meet you," he said.

"Brad was trying to get across a message. His life was shit."

He tipped his head to one side, looking puzzled, trying to reform the syllable he thought he had heard.

I said, "There's no point to it, Barbara, okay? They're suffering already, can't you let them suffer their own way?"

Barbara looked at me, looked around the room with its small pictures and isolated plates on the wall, so little different from the rooms in my mother's house. "Do you want me to participate in vanishing Brad? You know I can't do that." She bounded away across the room, bumping people and excusing herself too loudly, and I watched her until she made a sudden change of direction and found Brad's brother Billy, half-hidden in the window drapes. She spoke urgently to him, then the two of them disappeared into the interior of the house.

Well, I thought, there's one who's going to get Brad's message. I got coffee, circled the room, pretending I was on my way back to someone. I found myself at the wall with the three china plates again. They nagged at me: who had plates like that? Not my mother, but someone I knew. My aunt? My grandmother? But we would never have hung them on the wall, I thought. Stood them in a row on top of a hutch, maybe. But it didn't matter, this was still the house I'd always known. If I didn't run, I would end up in a house like this, in a town like my town. With dollhouse plates on a blank wall.

I turned away and bumped into Martha, who met my eyes coolly. "Where's your friend?"

"Giving Brad's message to Billy."

"Listen, you and your friend knew Brad—"

"Not really," I said. "I'm walking around here and I can't even remember what he looked like."

"Then you certainly don't know Phyllis. You don't know the family. Phyllis's husband, when Brad was in high school, died in a hunting accident."

"Killed himself?" I said.

"Shot himself," said Martha, not blinking. "No one knows the exact circumstances, but it was a great tragedy."

"That's grim." Martha gave me a chance to take it in, but I didn't mean to be taken in. I said, "There's no question about Brad, though, he really jumped."

"Phyllis had a nervous breakdown," said Martha. "Phyllis had a nervous breakdown over Brad's father, and this is too much. We don't intend to let her have another. So you see, nothing is simple, nothing is as simple as it appears when you're eighteen."

"Nineteen," I said. "Why shouldn't she have a breakdown if she wants to? If people on all sides of her are killing themselves, it seems logical to me." Saying this made me feel a little better: no one doomed to a small narrow life would ever say anything so outrageous.

Martha's face was more interesting when she didn't smile. "What do you want from me?" she said. "Evidence of stupidity or words of wisdom?"

Wisdom, I thought. Tell me how you can live out your life in Viola and tell me how someone like Phyllis can inspire you to so much love and tell me how you can stop another person from breaking down.

But Barbara was leading Billy back into the living room.

"Oh no," said Martha.

Barbara looked like an angel: her dark hair had spread out behind her, and the boy was so close that he seemed to have bloomed up out of it. "I told Billy," she said.

"Oh, Billy, honey." Martha reached for him, but he pulled back.

His eyes were red, and he had a couple of infected pimples on his cheeks, and tender skin just above his ears where his hair had recently been cut. "People should know," he said. "Brad deserves that much."

"That's what Barbara says," I said.

"Right," said Billy.

"And what about Phyllis?" asked Martha. "She deserves something, too."

Billy looked at Martha with childish accusation. "Brad had his hair long. If I'd of known that, I wouldn't have got mine cut for the funeral, I'll tell you that."

"Listen, Billy," said Martha. "The funeral was for your mother. That's who you cut your hair for, and all I ask is that you think of her a little longer. Can you leave her out of this? Okay, Billy?"

Barbara touched Billy's arm, and Martha's, linking them, and said, "We'll leave the rest of the people out of it, the ones who aren't strong enough. It's really all right. I understand, too."

Billy nodded solemnly. "My mom doesn't have to know."

Martha started to speak, but her smile twitched and her eyes seemed to bulge, and I realized she was about to cry. Now why does she have to do that? I thought. Why do people always do the thing you don't expect?

But then I had a gift: a memory of Brad as clear as I had ever seen him in life, probably clearer. Wearing crusty jeans and a black denim jacket with the sleeves cut off; his arms bare and little homemade blue ink tattoos of imaginary animals on his shoulders and biceps. He shook his head and his hair shifted, swung, came to rest.

And then I wondered: at the last moment, had he gone out onto the fire escape on impulse? Did he not even hesitate, but just jump? Or did he, perhaps, sit for a moment on the rusting crossbar, for one instant all of a piece, not scattered.

Choose, damn you, I thought. At least let it be that you chose.

He lifted both his hands and jumped.

I said to the others, "I finally remember what Brad looked like."

But Martha was on her way back to Phyllis, and Barbara was giving Billy her phone number, because, she said, she wanted to be there if he ever needed her. I watched Brad fall, a long way to the bottom.

True Romance

THE YELLOW INSECT-REPELLENT lights of the Custard Castle glittered against the rainy night. Inside, Pamela pressed her face to the plate glass and watched the florist's truck drive off. Geraldine said to her, "He'll be back."

"Darn straight he will. He's taking me home."

"Again?"

"Yes, again." Pamela glared belligerently until Geraldine went back to her love magazine, but that left Pam with nothing to do but pace between the serving windows.

The first night Rudy took her home she had been flattered; the second, third, and fourth nights she had been in love; last night he showed her a felt mattress he kept rolled up in the back of the truck among the wreaths.

She watched through the Custard Castle window as a car came over the bridge too fast for the slick asphalt; it skidded briefly, but recovered and ground gears down the highway. She was disappointed, wanting some catastrophe to fill the night: glass shattering, shrieks, a geyser of carbonated water from the root beer barrel. She had self-confidence in emergencies, thrived on fire drills and ambulance sirens. Anything but the yellow stillness of this glass pound. The thunderstorm had stopped business, and even the ice cream machine kicked off. The only sound was an irregular hum she couldn't place at first. It was Geraldine singing "Rock of Ages" under her breath.

"Can't you sing anything but hymns?"

Geraldine didn't look up. She chewed on a plastic spoon and traced her story with a finger down the magazine column. She was a born-again Pentecostal and a high school dropout, but she had a substantial chest and a tiny waist. She had a boyfriend, too, that she had met here at the Custard Castle. He had ambled down out of some hollow one day, with an overbite just like Geraldine's. Pamela imagined them breeding a toothy race of Holy Rollers. The boyfriend was in the army now, and Geraldine wrote him eleven-page letters every other day. The idea of an eleven-page letter from Geraldine bored her incredibly.

Pam rested her cheek on the green enamel milkshake mixer. "I smell sour milk. You better clean this gunk off the beaters before Iris gets here."

"Clean it yourself."

"Not me. I only get paid for wearing my skirt short and serving customers."

"Talk about your own self!"

"Ask Iris. She says Mr. Powers told her he would never hire boys to work in here because the customers like to look at girls, especially ones with nice shapes. I figure it was your bosom that got you the job, Geraldine. That, and because you read love magazines. To teach you how to do it—is that it?"

"You talk, Pamela Boatwright. If more girls read those stories, they'd think twice before they did some things."

Pamela wondered mildly if Iris had told Geraldine to say that when Pam got on her back. Iris scolded Pam for trying to shock people, but the truth was, Pam only liked to shock people like Geraldine because there wasn't much else to do with them. She much preferred working on Iris's nights. Iris, who had done everything already and couldn't be shocked. Pam would say, "Iris, tell me what I look like—tell me what you would think of me if you were a man." Iris had gray little eyes half-hidden behind her mascara and fake lashes.

"Well," she would say, "you're not the cuddly type, but you're an armful. You give off a certain impression, though, and it's going to get you in trouble one of these days."

"Oh, don't worry," Pam would say, "I just play."

She hoped Iris would come early tonight. Iris was closing the Castle while Mr. Powers was on vacation, and tonight Pam wasn't playing. She had some important questions she was going to try and ask: Does it ever hurt? Does there have to be blood? You can't get into trouble the first time, can you?

"Hey, Geraldine, what's your story about? Let me guess, somebody is regretting she did it, or else she's regretting she didn't do it when she had the chance."

"This girl got drunk and made a mistake with someone she hardly knows and she is trying to decide whether or not to tell her boyfriend who she really loves."

"That's easy. She should tell him, and if she doesn't like the way he reacts, she should be glad to be rid of him."

"You can say that, Pam, but when a person does wrong, a Christian person does wrong, it isn't so easy. A girl's whole life can be poisoned by remorse."

This was less boring. "Geraldine, tell me the truth. Do you ever get an itch to do it?"

Geraldine let her magazine fall and picked up the spills rag. The faint odor of Clorox tickled Pam's nose and there was an interesting redness on Geraldine's cheek.

Pam said, "Poor old Geraldine, I bet you know something about remorse. What was it like, the first time you did it with your soldier?"

Geraldine threw the rag. It was not really aimed at Pam, and she dodged it with no trouble, but it slapped against the ice cream machine and slithered into the milky drip pan under the serving heads.

"We're going to get married, and we thought he was going to Vietnam instead of Kansas!"

"You mean you really did it? I was teasing, Geraldine, I never thought you did it with him. You and your soldier actually did it?"

Geraldine ran for the back room with her shoulders hunched up. "Five times is all! We did it five times right before he left!"

"In one night?" Pam called after her. But she had a customer. Everyone does it, thought Pam, even Pentecostals. She put hot fudge on the sundae and slid it through the serving window. Geraldine now took on a new importance. Geraldine cared enough about something to throw wet rags and cry. Geraldine had done it.

After all the lights and chrome, the back of the Custard Castle was like a cave with its unpainted cinderblock walls and stacks of cardboard boxes and empty ten-gallon milk cans. Geraldine was crying as she rinsed rags in steaming Clorox water. How often, Pam wondered, do ordinary people do it? Once you get started, do you need a certain quota a week? "Listen, Geraldine, after all, you're in love. You were afraid he would never come back."

"It's no excuse. There's no excuse for doing what you know is forbidden."

"I suppose you couldn't control yourselves."

"I shouldn't have let myself get into that situation. It's my fault for letting myself be tempted."

"Were you out parked in his car?"

"No, in the front room. My parents were at church."

"On the couch?"

"Under the table."

"Under the table? But what about the table legs? I mean, where did you lie down? That's what beds are for, Geraldine, if you're in the house, anyhow!"

"I told you, we didn't plan it. I kept getting tempted, and then I would sort of slide down, and he kept sliding with me."

TV sets, thought Pamela. A needlepoint hassock. Reader's Digest. And people copulating under all the dining room tables. Bathtubs, too, she supposed. In offices, in the back room of the Custard Castle. In a florist's delivery truck.

The key turned in the lock, and Iris came in, wearing pink stretch slacks and a sleeveless sweater, her hair freshly set and teased. She had her baby with her, dresssed up in pink dotted swiss, miniature patent leather slippers and a tiny charm bracelet. "Good evening," said Iris, looking them over with her eyebrows raised. She set her baby carefully on a case of chocolate syrup. "I didn't see anybody in the front. I thought you two'd abandoned ship. Come and look at Kimmie Dawn's new bracelet."

Pam stepped aside to let Geraldine run at the baby. "It's crazy here tonight, Iris. People are doing it all over the place. People keep mattresses in the back of their cars so they can do it if the mood strikes them."

Geraldine kissed Kimmie Dawn's fingernails. "In the back of their *panel* trucks, she means."

"Under their dining room tables, she means! She threw a rag at me, Iris. Geraldine got so mad she threw a rag. It was about sex."

Iris retied a pink ribbon on one of Kimmie Dawn's little pony-tails. "The bracelet is a gift from my old man. He never brings me a thing, but he just piles presents on Kimmie Dawn. He was over for dinner tonight, and he offered to babysit, but I said, 'My baby goes where I go, unless she stays with my mom.'"

Kimmie Dawn was illegitimate, and Iris had never told who the father was, although it was supposed to be a well-known man in the community.

"See that little rocking horse charm, Pammie?"

Pam grunted. She didn't like it when Iris got sentimental over Kimmie Dawn's little outfits.

"I never saw anything so cute," said Geraldine. "But Pam's not interested. All she's interested in is Rudy Conway."

"Rudy Conway? Is that the truth, Pammie?" Iris's face compressed into toughness. That was the way Pam liked her.

"He's taking her home again. He's been over here three times tonight already drinking root beer floats, so he says."

"What is that supposed to mean, Geraldine, 'So he says'? You either drink a root beer float or you don't," said Pam. "And that's right, Rudy is giving me a lift home."

Geraldine said, "She wouldn't listen to me, Iris, but I think someone should talk to her."

"You get Kimmie Dawn a ice cream cone, Geraldine. Put a towel around her neck first." Iris folded a clean towel for herself on the lid of a milk can. Her feet didn't touch the floor, so she crossed one thigh over the other, and crossed her arms under her breasts. She lowered her chin severely. "Pammie, you have a lot of advantages in your life. You're a school principal's daughter. You've got college written all over you. I hope you aren't as careless as you talk."

Pam said, "Hey, Iris, you got a new bra, didn't you? It's really pointed."

Iris had a trick of holding her face perfectly still so that you couldn't tell if she was mad or amused or choosing not to hear. "You're going to go to the university, you and Tommy, together. Now, how would you feel if Tommy walked in here tonight and found you planning to let Rudy Conway take you home?"

"I'd feel bored. Tommy is boring. He'll be working at his stupid camp all summer, and I could care less."

"Did you break up with him?"

"Not exactly. But I'm going to. Tommy is the last thing on my mind."

"If I ever found Kimmie Dawn going out with an older man, I would beat her black and blue. I mean it. Girls and men have different things on their minds. I should know what happens when a young girl gets mixed up with a man."

"Oh, Iris, everyone has the same thing on their mind. Even Geraldine. Being young and innocent just means you want it and you don't know how to get it."

"Aren't we talking big this evening."

"Listen, I read about this South Sea Island where, when you reach a certain age, they assign you an older man for a weekend, and you go off with him, and he teaches you everything. All your questions get answered."

Iris didn't blink for several seconds, then she pointed. "Hand me my bag. I'll just go ahead and crochet while you tell me stories about cannibals."

"Don't get mad, Iris. I need you to answer my questions. All I want to know is what it's like, that's all. Tell me about your first time, Iris."

"None of your goddam business. Excuse my French. The only thing that counts is to take care of yourself. You hang on to Tommy. He'll be a lawyer one of these days like his father."

"I'd rather have his father—at least he's got some hair on his body. I'll tell you what, I'll put Tommy in the freezer and you can save him for Kimmie Dawn if you think he's so great."

Iris became absorbed in her crocheting, then spoke. "What happened to me should be lesson enough for any girl. I worshipped that man. Any queer thing he wanted, I begged for the privilege."

Pam leaned her elbows on the carton next to Iris; she loved this. She wanted Iris's voice to slip right into her head and down her spine. She whispered, "What kind of queer things?"

"None of your damn business."

"How did he get you to do it the first time?"

"How did he get me to do it? I'm telling you, I was ready. There wasn't any first time—I was so ready I would have done it to him. He stayed with me two years because he knew a good thing when he saw it. Free and enthusiastic. Until Kimmie Dawn got started, and he was off like a shot."

"Why didn't you get a lead pipe and beat his head in?"

Iris twisted and knotted her violet yarn, locking loop into loop. "He tried to give me money. But the one thing he wouldn't do was get a divorce and marry me, so I said, 'Let it be.'"

"You mean to tell me you broke up with him? You got pregnant and then you broke up with him? And you tell me to get smart and plan for the future?"

"I did okay without his help. I take pretty damn good care of my baby for someone with no education. I don't take anything from my old man either. Even-Steven with him. I take care of my own self and Kimmie Dawn."

Pam thought the answer to all her problems would be if Iris could just turn into a man for a while, a small blond man with those same quick hands. A man who knew the score the way Iris did, a man who would play Pamela like a guitar, and her body would sing and never be bored.

"Take one piece of advice, Pam. Stay away from Rudy Conway. I know him, and he isn't honest with you."

Geraldine came creeping back, pretending to help Kimmie Dawn walk.

"Well, maybe I'm not being honest with him either. What do you know about Rudy?"

"I went to school with him."

It passed through Pam's mind that Rudy had been Iris's first old man, Kimmie Dawn's father, but Rudy would be too young, the same age as Iris.

"The best thing that could happen to you right now would be if Tommy came home. Cover Kimmie Dawn's ears, Geraldine. If Tommy came home and straightened out your ass."

Geraldine giggled.

"Tommy had better never try. Tommy or Rudy Conway either." She had an exhilarating vision of a fight with Rudy. They would slap one another with mops, throw melting handfuls of ice cream. She imagined lifting a ten-gallon milk jug over her head and throwing it, and a plate-glass window would shatter and cool air rush in. The lights go off and her body and Rudy's collide over and over again. "Tell me about Rudy."

"I didn't say I had anything to tell you about Rudy. What do you think of my little hat, Geraldine? It's going to be a cloche, with a ribbon running in and out along here."

"You had better tell me, Iris. I have to know."

"So, you think you really like Rudy?"

"I don't know. I'm deciding."

Geraldine hissed, "Well, you better decide quick, because here he comes again."

She wasn't ready yet, but she thrust her hands in her pockets to pull the uniform tight over her behind and sauntered to the serving window.

"Evening, Geraldine," called Rudy. "Hello back there, Miss Iris. It's been a long time."

"That's not my fault." Iris stayed in the doorway. "I'm not the one who went off to Detroit and hasn't been back."

"Well, I'm back now."

"How's your family?"

"Oh, Dad has his good days and his bad days. I'm taking care of the flower business till he gets on his feet."

Pam leaned on the counter. Because of the advertising posters on the window, all she could see of Rudy through the little serving door was his hands folding and unfolding a dollar bill.

"Have you seen my little girl, Rudy? Kimberly Dawn, walk up there; I want that man to take a look at you."

Kimmie Dawn tottered around the ice cream machine and leaned to one side to see Rudy, then she ran back.

"That was real cute; you've got a real cute little girl, Iris."

"Spoiled rotten," said Iris, and they kept on calling to one another over the ice cream machines like neighbors over the back hedge.

Pam was getting bored and started to walk away, but Rudy's arm shot in through the wicket all the way to the shoulder, and he seized her by the wrist and jerked her in front of him, saying, "Hey, what do you have to do to get waited on around here? I want a coke."

Pam made a fist and struck his arm hard. "Let go of me before I punch your teeth in."

He released her at once. "What's the matter with you? I never saw a pretty face get so ugly."

"It's my face."

"Who wants it?"

"You can't just grab me when you want me when you didn't speak to me for ten minutes."

Geraldine chose to empty the drip tray then, and she paused with her mouth open.

Pam stamped. "Get out of here, Geraldine. This isn't television."

"You've got a real mean streak, haven't you?" said Rudy, bending over to see her without the screen or the glass. "I was only playing."

"I wasn't."

"So I see. I thought you liked games." That was to make her think of the seat of the van and how he held her down and said she was driving him crazy, and how she struggled to get free, but with her thighs.

His arms came in again, with one finger extended, and he touched very lightly the point of bare skin where her dress buttoned. "I apologize for being rough."

"I just don't let anyone act like they own me. I haven't done anything to give you any rights over me."

"That's for sure." The button on her uniform had come undone, and he buttoned it. "I wouldn't mind having some rights over you."

"No one," she said. The point on her breastbone he had touched burned. "Especially no man." She scanned his face to see if he thought she was making a fool of herself.

"That's right. Nobody has any rights over you but you." He started laughing and shaking his head, and his eyes flicked over her.

"Go ahead and laugh." It was all right as long as he laughed to her face; she could tell where she stood.

"Just the same, I wish I did." His skin was coarse. He had many textures—rough cheeks, curly hair at the throat, silky arm hair. Tommy was an egg except for the fuzz on his legs and lip. Almost seventeen and not even shaving yet. The wind shifted slightly, carrying in Rudy's odor, and a shiver passed over Pam's shoulders. The first time they kissed had been in his truck. She had at once distinguished his scent from the crumbling leather dust and the funeral flowers: penetrating, distinct. Rudy smelled mildly of sweat, and of skin oils. Nothing spicy, no hair cream or aftershave. Solid, unique, the odor of Rudy's flesh.

"I'll get your coke," she said.

When she dropped his change, she left her hand on the counter. It was almost as long as his, but more slender, and apricot-colored. She couldn't decide whose hand was more beautiful.

He said softly, "I grant you I have no right, but the problem is, I have to watch myself all the time because I don't want to make a mistake and have you run off."

She rotated her hand to rub the back of his with the back of hers. "I have to watch myself a little, too."

Her cheeks warmed up, and a sphere of warmth moved down the back of her neck through her inner body, activating limbs and organs until she felt alight and restless, ready to dive from a high place. Rudy's eyes were half shut, and in his smile his teeth showed.

He didn't leave right away, but yelled for Iris again, and she came to the window. Iris and Rudy talked a little about old times, and Pam listened indulgently, as if they were her parents telling stories about before she was born. The center on that great basketball team when we were freshmen, how he died in a mine cave-in, not even enough of a disaster to make the papers outside the county.

Rudy said he had one late delivery, and then he'd be back in half an hour to pick her up. Iris went back to her crocheting. Pam followed, suspended in an excitement that blurred the periphery of her vision.

"Iris, what I want to know is, is it really an ordinary everyday thing, or does something amazing happen?" And if there's power, she thought, who gets it, you or the man? Who wins, Iris?

Iris settled her behind on the milk can. "So you and Rudy Conway think you have something going."

"Answer me, Iris."

"What do you like about Rudy?"

"I don't know. The way he smells."

"I swear to God, Pammie. Well, see how you like the way this smells. When I asked about his family, I didn't mean his father and his heart attack. I meant his wife and kids in Detroit. Did he tell you he's married and has a family?"

Geraldine had crept in again, and nodded smartly with her lips pursed. Iris had a look of satisfaction, too, a settled jowliness. Pam squared her shoulders. "Well, I notice it didn't stop you from flirting with him."

"Don't try and get me mad, Pam, because I doubt you could handle it. Rudy is just doing what any normal man would do if he had a chance to go out with a pretty girl like you. Besides, it isn't as bad as it sounds. His sister tells me that he and his wife are having a bad time. In fact, he moved out a couple of months before his dad got sick."

"Why didn't you say that right off?"

"I wanted you to think a little bit. He never told you he had a family to support, did he?"

"He never even told her he was married."

"Geraldine, you stay out of it or I swear I'll call up your preacher and tell him about the table."

"Go on, revile and persecute me. I pray for them that despitefully use me."

"Pammie, all I'm saying is, you can do better than a man who works in a factory and has a family to support. You're going to meet someone when you go to the university. You'll see."

"I don't want to marry him, Iris! Why does everyone always think you're planning to marry someone?"

Iris looked to her crocheting and Geraldine picked up Kimmie Dawn; Kimmie Dawn whined to be let down. Iris said, "Sometimes you just can't talk to her."

Pam said, "Hey, Iris, did you used to go out with Rudy?"

"What makes you think that?"

"Because you showed off Kimmie Dawn to him—that means you like someone."

"Well, I told you I knew him. We went places together, just having fun. It wasn't like love."

She wondered if they had done it together. "I don't mind, you know. I like both of you. That's how I want him, too, just to have fun with."

"Rudy's a grown man and too old to play with."

"If he knew I knew about his wife and kids, would he feel bad?"

"I guess he's a little bit worried right now about what I know and how much I'm telling you. Yes, Rudy would feel bad."

"I won't tell him you told me. I may tease him about going out with you, though." She wouldn't tell him unless she had to, unless he began to use power against her. In the meantime, she would tease him, say, I know a secret about you, Rudy. Little worry wrinkles would show up around the corners of his eyes, and then she would say, Yes, Iris told me that you and she used to go out together. He would sigh with relief, and all the time she would be holding the real secret in reserve, behind her eyes, under her tongue, just in case she ever had to fight him.

Iris said, "You'll be careful, won't you, Pammie?"

"I'll be careful. I'm learning how to take care of myself."

"I doubt it. Get me my pocketbook. I want to fix up your hair if you're going out tonight."

"What's wrong with my hair?"

"You'll see. I had this idea for a long time, to pull your hair back."

She let Iris brush her hair. She felt the brushing all through her scalp and down her back and into her organs again.

"Pammie." Iris laid her fingers on Pam's eyelids, held them closed and whispered. "Now don't take this wrong, Pammie, but Rudy is a responsible man, and don't you let him do anything without taking precautions. There's no excuse for not taking precautions. Do you hear me?"

Pam smiled and nodded. Iris pulled back the hair on either side of her face and tied it with a piece of pink velvet ribbon from her purse. She had a travel-size cologne, too, and dabbed some behind Pam's ears and on her inner wrists. "Look at those fingernails. I swear. And you didn't think to bring a change of clothes." She whipped the apron off Pam, and Pam began to giggle. "Still, with an ass like that, even a uniform doesn't look bad."

Kimmie Dawn started to giggle along with Pam. Iris ignored the giggling and muttered to herself, pulling Pam to her and fussing over the loose button on Pam's bosom. For Pam, it was enough that Iris approved of how she looked. She had been straightened and dabbed and brushed. She thought she would like to stay between Iris's thighs when she did it. With Iris's hand all over her head and face. She decided that when she was with Rudy, she would carry Iris with her; Iris and Rudy when they were teenagers. Iris as she was now, too, with her old man, trying to pretend for good luck that they didn't like each other so much. "Okay, get out of here," said Iris, pushing her away. "And don't do anything I wouldn't do."

Yes, Pam thought, as she walked toward the door—a bit dazed and warm, but confident—she would take poor dumb Geraldine and her soldier, too, and herself and Tommy, and Rudy and his wife. She would cushion herself with all the people, all of them doing it around her in a great concert.

Evenings with
Dotson

I REMEMBER THOSE SUMMERS when Dotson used to visit me at my grandmother's as dark green and rank with Virginia Creeper. High Gap, where my grandmother had her store, was a row of mailboxes with a church across the creek and a one-room school overlooking the road. I loved the sudden rises and drops of mountainside and the slat-sided houses with their porches on stilts and their backsides pressed against the incline of the mountain. There were people, according to my grandmother, who lived so far up the hollows that there were no roads, only paths; people who came down once a year to buy goods at her store; people who never came down.

If you took the hardtop down the mountain, you came to a real town, named Pound because the Indians used to impound their horses there, and that was where you could find a drugstore, a dentist, and the high school Dotson attended. Pound became famous as the hometown of Francis Gary Powers, the U-2 spy pilot, but when I spent summers with my grandmother, he was known only as a local boy who made a good career in the Air

Force. The military was considered prime employment in that part of the world; and the Air Force, the best of the services. Something about the mountains must have made the boys want to go even higher: Dotson's uncle owned a Piper Cub, and Dotson talked about flying all the time.

It amazed me, the summer I was twelve and Dotson fourteen, that my grandmother didn't refuse to let him visit me. He arrived at dusk with his hair wet, wearing a white shirt and slacks, and my grandmother invited him in for a glass of iced tea. He answered her questions about his mother and little brothers with attentive respect, and then she sent us to sit on the concrete steps of the back porch, overlooking the creek and the Freewill Baptist Church. I remember the heaviness and dampness of the air, and something sweet-smelling that Dotson wore on his cheeks and neck. He talked about playing football, and I boasted about what my town had that Pound didn't: the public library and municipal swimming pool. I told him about the books I'd read, and he told me I was different from other girls and promised to take me up in an airplane. Then my grandmother turned off the television and started walking around the kitchen, flashing lights on and off until Dotson stood up crisply and said good-bye.

WE DIDN'T KISS until the next summer, when I was thirteen and his shoulders seemed to have doubled in width. He never wore overalls anymore, and he was more proud of his football letter than of his ability to hunt squirrels. He still loved best, though, to go up with his uncle and take the controls of the Piper Cub. That's when you know who you are, he said. That's when you feel like you could do anything.

The kiss came three nights after he told me a story about the boys in town. He liked to laugh about the practical jokes the town boys pulled and what they said to each other. This particular story concerned some black people who had driven through Pound in an old car that didn't look like it would make it over the next mountain. "Well," said Dotson, "there was no question of *whether* the boys was going to get them out of town, it was only a question of *how* they was going to do it." So what the boys did, said Dotson, was when the car stopped for the light, they just sort of surrounded it, and then leaned in the windows and stared. Then one of the boys said, real softly, "Y'all ain't planning on *stopping* here?" Like they were almost being polite. "Y'all ain't planning on *visiting* here long, are you? Because, you know, it ain't healthy after dark, not for y'all, that folks can't see after the sun goes down." Well, said Dotson, they were so scared they just peeled out, didn't even wait for the light to change, just took out of Pound and that was the last of them anyone saw around town. He gave a big Hoo Hoo and hit his leg with the heel of his hand. "That must of been something to see," he said.

I didn't say a word at first, just like the town boys leaning on the car. I waited till Dotson had hooted and snorted and finally settled down. All summer we had been having half-flirtatious, half-rivalrous debates over our towns and high schools and football teams and marching bands and cheerleading uniforms.

Dotson usually deferred to my opinion in the end, but I had begun to suspect him of humoring me, as if in his heart he knew that my arguments weren't going to convince him of anything, but he liked to make me happy.

For this reason, I was thankful for his story, delighted to feel firm ground under me, to take a stand. For the moment, the soaring black mountains were mine and Dotson was down in the muggy valley. "Dotson Otis," I said, "you sound like you're proud of what those boys did."

He stirred on the steps. He had perhaps expected a giggle or a tsk tsk of disapproval. I said, "Dotson, if somebody passing through High Gap came and asked you for a glass of water, wouldn't you give it to them? Wouldn't you give them directions if they were lost or a piece of bread if they were hungry? I mean, what if it was your mother or your little brother in a strange town? What if there was a car accident and those people in that strange town said, 'You can't use our hospital?'"

Dotson said, "But those were niggers. I explained that. They were *colored*."

I remember the control I felt over my voice, as if I were making a speech I had practiced for a long time. How I felt righteousness like a mantle around my shoulders. "Those were people in that car, Dotson," I said. "And you shouldn't use that word for people. They were just people driving through and maybe needing to get something to drink or a sandwich or some gasoline. And those boys you think so much of denied them, and if you deny even the Least of These My Brethren, you are doing it to Jesus, he said so himself in the Bible."

Dotson seemed a little stunned to have Bible quoted at him. I think he saw it as his people guarding the passes against outsiders. I think that's what the story meant to him. But I didn't give him a chance to restate it, I just moved on from Jesus to Thomas Jefferson.

I said, "In this country the Declaration of Independence says people are created equal and they have a right to drive their cars where they want and go to school where they want and live their lives just as free as you and me. Didn't you ever hear of the Supreme Court?"

Dotson got a little sullen. "They have places to live. They should stay there."

"Those people were driving through your town, Dotson Otis," I said. "That's all they were doing. And your friends treated them like dirt."

We sat with dew falling on our faces and knees, and the cold coming through our pants from the concrete steps. Abruptly he stood up and said, "Well, I guess I better be going." It was the first time he didn't wait for my grandmother's noises.

He's prejudiced, I said to myself, feeling lonely, but proud.

He didn't come in the store for two days, but on the third day he went through the whole ritual again of hanging around drinking Pepsi till late, then finally asking my grandmother for permission to come over. The nights had begun to cool, almost time for my parents to come and get me. He sat with his knees separated and his hands clasped between them, his head lowered.

"I've been thinking," he said. "I decided to think over what you said, and I've been thinking about it for three days, and like you said, the Declaration of Independence and all. Now, I don't mean I want them living next to me, but I can see where they should of been able to stop and buy gas or a Pepsi. Anyhow, I decided our boys were wrong."

His voice got deeper and softer as he said this, and I found myself overawed that he had spent three days thinking about something. I tended to take things literally at that age, and I imagined that he had thought for the full three days.

"Now, don't get me wrong about one thing," he said. "I doubt I would have done a thing to stop them if I'd been there, because they're my friends. But I think you're right and they were wrong."

I meant to scold him for not putting his new belief into action, but I let it go, let the argument run out into the enormous sounds of the creek battering its stones and the mountains singing with crickets. And Dotson asked me—with a politeness so profound I absolutely believed he would have accepted a no as easily as a yes—if he could kiss me. I presented my face and opened my mouth, and when he found the open mouth, his whole body stirred, and waves of sweet-smelling lotion passed over me. I am thirteen years old, I thought, and I am tongue-kissing for the first time.

"I want to take you up in a plane," he said into my ear. "I want to take you up in a plane and show you the mountains."

DOTSON FINALLY DID take me up in an airplane, but he didn't show me the mountains. I was a sophomore at Barnard College in New York City, and the Air Force was about to send him overseas. He called me from Teterboro Airport across the river in New Jersey to say he'd just flown up in his uncle's new Cessna, and he wanted to take me out for an early dinner and a sunset flight to see the Manhattan skyline.

I had classes the next day, and I hadn't seen Dotson since high school. I knew from my grandmother he was married, but I'd just had a fight with my boyfriend, and there was an air of adventure about the whole thing. Besides, I told myself, this was a unique opportunity to try and convince someone not to fight in that war.

The New Jersey restaurant he chose had red carpets and chairs with upholstered arms and lights that hung from wagon wheels. We were so early that we were the only customers, and he insisted on ordering both of us the Steak King Platter with the potato and garlic bread and sour cream and cheesecake. He sat back in his chair and said, "I like this place. I have a good feeling about it. I predict the steaks will be as thick as the cushions."

The thing that amazed me was how he looked the same as he had at fourteen: very white, head and shoulders too big for his body, the long jaw, the thick forearms, and the stubbly hair that exposed his scalp. So familiar, and yet so unlike most of the boys I knew. We liked our men hairy in those days: sideburns, mustaches, even ponytails. I said, "I've been eating in a lot of Chinese and Italian restaurants lately."

He grinned. "Then you must be ready for a steak."

I had a feeling anything I said was going to be all right with him. It made it hard to get up a controversy. I told him more about the restaurants and different styles of food in New York. I tried to convince him of how wonderful New York was, and why I intended to live there forever. He listened; he smiled at whatever I said; he remained unconvinced.

He said, "Me, I've had too much dormitory food, and who knows what slop they'll feed us over there."

"When are you leaving?" I was trying to work my way into my subject.

He looked at his hands longer than seemed necessary. "Soon," he said, and abruptly began to talk. I had somehow thought he'd invited me to hear my message, but he had things to tell me. He told how he had suffered at his military college the first year, how homesick he had been for High Gap and Pound, even becoming physically ill, throwing up every morning when they sounded reveille. Losing weight, hating the other cadets, the rich men's sons from the suburbs of Richmond and Washington. How, even with enormous effort, he had come as close as possible to flunking out yet still staying in.

He hated the regulations, too, the uniforms and Yessirs and salutes and stiff backs, but, sometime during the second year, he had begun to feel less alone, to understand that everyone hated the same things. He began to feel that what he was going through was something he did for the other cadets, as well as for the people back home. Little by little, he began to feel the man that the discipline was shaping him into, just the same as you could feel your own biceps thickening over time from lifting weights. He felt this knotty, disciplined core of an officer maturing inside him. "I'm ready for responsibility now," he told me. "I bought a piece of property up on High Gap. I want to build a house when I get back."

The salads came. I said, "You and Margaret Lee."

He touched his lower lip with a thumb. "We got married. I didn't know whether you knew or not."

"I heard. Does she know you came up here?"

He looked me straight in the eye: an act of discipline, I thought. "No. She thinks my uncle and I flew to Canada to go fishing. I would never of done something like this behind her back, except I wasn't sure you would come and see me. I wanted to make sure I saw you one last time."

It flattered me, and reminded me that he was going to be in danger, too. That his faintly freckled forearms, his thick wrists and square hands, his painstakingly cleaned nails—that this Dotson was going to be strapped into a little airplane with missiles coming at him, dropping from him.

I wanted to make it simple, to shout: Don't endanger yourself, Dotson! Just don't go over there. Don't drop the bombs.

And have him simply nod: I'll think it over, maybe you're right.

But dinner came, and I had to compliment the steak, and Dotson sighed his satisfaction. "The property is way back up on High Gap. Farther up than your grandmother's store. Margaret Lee is having the site graded this summer. We're going to build a brick house."

I could imagine it: I'd seen the solid brick houses with aluminum awnings in clearings up there, half a mile from shanties with no running water. It would be their cousins in the shanties: you built your good house near your people, that was the way it was done.

"I'm going to be a father, too," said Dotson. "I've had a hard time, but I feel like I'm coming out the other side now. Even if something happens over there, Margaret Lee and that baby will be taken care of."

"A baby," I said. "A baby and a house on High Gap."

"There's no better place. I can't think of anywhere I'd rather go back to. Or fight for."

I was finally moved to speak.

"You know, Dotson, your place—High Gap, Pound—that's home to you. I mean, where you were born and where you want to go back and live? And you say you'd fight for it."

"You bet," said Dotson. "That's America. That's my home. That's why we're over there, to fight for it."

"But the people over there, Dotson, in Vietnam and Laos and Cambodia—*We're* the ones destroying their homes."

He shook his head slowly. "We're fighting to help them hold the line against the Communists."

"No, Dotson. We take them out of their villages and make them go live in refugee camps and cities, and you can imagine how country people like that. They prefer the Communists to us. The Communists are their own people. We're the invaders over there."

Almost to himself he said, "I'm glad to hear this. This may be my only chance to ever hear this."

I said, "Doesn't it make any sense to you, what I'm saying?"

"I'll tell you the truth, it sounds strange to me. It sounds like you're on the Communists' side. But I just want to listen to you for now. You go ahead." He leaned forward, arms on the table, head to one side.

I took a deep breath. "We're supporting a dictator who puts his own people in jail if they disagree with him. It's a civil war, and it's none of our business."

"Now, I don't know," said Dotson. "I don't know as much as you do. I'm an officer and a flyer. What I see happening over there is that it's the first step of an enemy who'd like to take away my little place on High Gap. The way I look at it is, if somebody came up to High Gap and aimed a gun at me, I'd fight, and this gun is just farther away. I know the Air Force is going to tell me things to keep my morale up, and I don't suppose every word of it will be true, but I've signed on. I trust them in the long run that the missions they send me on will protect my home and my family."

The thing that astounded me, the thing that left me with no ground under my feet, was that he and I were envisioning the same thing—the brick house on High Gap and a new baby— that we could both see this, and yet he thought he was fighting to save it and I thought he was destroying it.

He must have seen something stricken in my face, because he touched me for the first time, tapped my elbow with one finger. "Listen, it's okay. It's a free country."

I had a sensation like a child who is given something sweet to eat when there is a pain in her body. The touch reminded me of his easy, time-consuming kisses, and at the same time I saw him, for a moment, with a mask over his face before a bank of flashing buttons, his voice cracking over a radio: "Payload Number One deployed," he would say. "Ready Payload Number Two." I imagined tons of clinging fire, on trees, on the round heads of children. I thought of those things, but they kept fading to Dotson with his shiny stubble of hair, his squinted eyes when he smiled.

"Did you come to get tested?" I said. "Am I part of your officer training?"

He stroked my arm. "I just wanted to be sure I saw you one last time. It's my way of preparing, as best I can."

I laid my hand on his, worked my way up his forearm. The skin cool on top, the muscle underneath rounded and hard like something machine tooled. The steel they'd made inside him, I reminded myself. How they'd brainwashed him. But not just the Air Force, also what they told him on the football field, his friends at Pound. It wasn't anything new, it was just more of the same old thing.

He said, "Let me take you in the plane now."

I went with him, passive in the face of his conviction, a power that came from both of us knowing he might die. I let him pay the bill, drive me to the airport. I followed him down the row of planes, stood back as he checked over the Cessna, looked under the wings, turned the propeller by hand. I was reminded dreamily that this white thing was only a machine, that machines have to be maintained or they'll break down. Reminded that I was trusting him to take me up and set me down safely.

He flipped switches, tugged at my safety belt, tested his gauges,

tucked his chin, and then the engine, the propellers, and a familiar sensation of rolling on the ground—followed by a sudden
heady absence of friction, and we were flying, over the ranks of
blue, yellow, and white planes, over New Jersey roofs, over cars
creeping on an expressway. A sweep around, the domination of
the George Washington Bridge with its green night-lights just
coming on.

My breath came rapidly, and I began to revive from my pas-
sivity, to feel a little of the flush of power that comes from danger. I shouted, "You pilots like to risk your lives, don't you, in
these little tin cans?"

He laughed; it was the first time we had teased each other all
evening.

"I never feel as safe as when I'm flying," he said. "It's beautiful,
isn't it?"

We were flying south along the Hudson River. New York on
our left, lit both by electricity and by a sunset that turned bricks
and concrete gold and pink, made windows flash. We weren't
very high; some of the tallest buildings were higher than we
were, and the river seemed vastly more broad than I had ever
supposed. I could look down the canyons of streets for an instant
as we passed. At midtown, the glitter of the skyscrapers seemed
to overwhelm even the sunset. Dotson tipped the wings so I
could see better, and again I felt the rush of adrenaline, understood what he loved.

We flew over the bay. Fat yellow ferry leaving its berth. We
began another maneuver, tipping in my direction this time, exe-
cuting a complete circle, a turn on a dime, and a hundred feet

directly below me was the upraised arm of the Statue of Liberty and the spikes around her huge head.

"It's beautiful, Dotson!" I shouted. "It's so beautiful!"

He circled the statue once more, at a slightly greater height, and then started back up the river. "This is the way I like to see a city," he said. "I like a view of it, but I don't like to be in it."

This city, I thought, amazed by the way it filled my eyes. This city is one whole thing. And I live here. But a single target, too; a terrorist could bomb this city. I looked at Dotson, who knew how to bomb, whose profile had a ruddy aura from the sun, whose jaw stretched deliberately as he surveyed what was below him.

"Dotson!" I shouted, and I laid my hand on his shoulder. "Dotson! Listen to me. Don't go over there. If you go over there, you're going to kill people. There's no way it will make it anything but worse."

Damp-faced, half-laughing, he shrugged my hand off his shoulder, then grabbed it up with his and squeezed it.

"Come on, Dotson," I said. "This is so beautiful. No wonder you love to fly. I don't want to go down. Let's keep flying. Let's fly this thing to Canada!" I meant it, too, at least for that moment. I felt perfectly free: I could go to Canada as easily as back to college. "It would be easy, Dotson!" I shouted. "You can find Canada. *I* could practically find Canada. Just go up the Hudson River. How long could it take from here? Two hours? Just go north. Margaret Lee can come too, they have good hospitals in Canada. It's a nice country, Dotson. I'm right, Dotson, you know I'm right!"

I think, at that moment, in his favorite place, with the world laid out underneath us, George Washington Bridge looming ahead, I think he was as close to agreeing with me as he ever would be.

"You're really something," he said. "You make deserting sound like this great thing to do." I leaned over and turned my face to him, and he kissed me, and I felt desire in a swelling wave that would carry us all the way to Canada.

But the plane tipped. Not a lot, just enough that Dotson had to take action. Had to stop kissing and do what he was trained to do. When he had righted us, he was still flushed and laughing, but amusement had become stronger than the wave.

"What if I say you're right?" he said. "What if I say you're maybe right, but in a dream, and I'm in the real world. I'm in the real world with real Communists and the Air Force and commitments."

"That's the old world," I said, perceiving a sudden heaviness, pain in the precision of detail in the hard-edged skyline.

"Yes," said Dotson, "that's the way it's always been."

I have never been sorry for anything that happened between me and Dotson that night. I would have been far sorrier if, in some other life, I had not spent the night with him. And he was very wise to say good-bye to old friends, because he did not come back from Asia. He was shot down over Cambodia. I hope he was able to believe in his final fiery moments that he was protecting his home on High Gap. And I hope his final moments were indeed fiery and not at the hands of some bitter farmers who saw him as the destroyer of their High Gap. I hope they did not visit on his tight, white body the rage of their loss.

The Trestle

I DREAM I AM walking on the railroad tracks across a trestle, far above the valley floor. Dragonflies are hovering; sometimes a bird passes; you can see the thick tufty green of the treetops through the spaces between the ties.

In the distance, the train whistles as it approaches town. I hurry, although there is more than enough time to get safely across. I try not to take steps that are too big for the little girl with me. Even so, the little girl stumbles, and her foot slips between two of the closely spaced ties. Quickly I stoop to reassure her and free the foot; it seems we could get it out easily if we took off the shoe, but her ankle blows up fat and salmon pink, and in spite of sawing the foot back and forth, I can't get it free.

The train whistles at the junction, less than a mile away. I hear it, but it still sounds far off, as do the little girl's wails, several in quick succession, the same pattern as the train. Only ten yards behind me is a platform with a water barrel. I hear the chugging of the train now and have a glimpse of black through the trees. In a few seconds we'll see the teeth of the cowcatcher head on, and the engineer will try to stop, but he will be going much too fast. It is already too late. Like the ankle, the little girl's face is swollen and ugly with screaming. I find myself backing away to save myself. I am aware this is not the right thing to do. The little girl spreads her arms begging. I know that the right thing would be to keep the little girl company. The locomotive is on the trestle now, bristling with smoke and metal, whistling and screeching as it tries to stop. The clamor is distasteful. I am furious with the unfairness of the right thing to do.

Below, the air seems thick as water, and some birds swim by without a sound, dipping and swooping. The green tufted bedspread would like to enfold me and mother me. I make a perfect three-step approach and dive off the trestle. I somersault slowly over and over in the green air, feeling the sun.

June's Legacy

J UNE ONCE TOLD her daughter a dream she had of frying hamburgers after the moving van had taken away the furniture. The family was gone, and she was the only one left in the house. Tears ran down her face. "It was so sad," June said, "to fry hamburgers when no one was coming."

J UNE WAS TEN YEARS OLD, the youngest in her family, born when her own mother was already ill, when the family was forced to break up because her father was laid off. He went where there was work; her mother got a live-in job cleaning for a family in the next town. June was sent to live with a cousin who was married and about to have a baby, hours away through the mountains by Model T, even farther by the B & O, through all the whistle-stop company towns that cluster along the ice-edged rivers and black railroads.

Her cousin's husband Robey was a man who explained that he worked for the company in a managerial capacity. He wore a suit every day and intended to make something big of himself. Robey made June's cousin take off her apron before sitting down to supper, then complained that there were lumps in the mashed potatoes. He preferred tomato ketchup mixed into the meat loaf rather than spread on top.

June did not make friends at once. She had to walk home from school alone. One bright winter afternoon, the man who kept the store was standing on the boardwalk, and he waved and waved to her. She went near, and he showed a long paper strip with little bright colored candies glued lightly to it. "Buttons," he said.

She didn't have any money.

"I'll trade you buttons," he said, and he gestured again. She stepped in out of the sun into the dark of the store. The man sat on a box and pulled her close to him and rubbed her cheek with his. "Mmm, good," he said. Then he reached under her coat and felt her chest. "See," he said, "Buttons for buttons."

She waited for someone to come and save her, but no one did, so she finally pulled away from the man and ran for home. Her cousin was out, no one in the house but Robey, who had a cold and was wearing his dressing gown with an undulating paisley print. She ran into the little room where she slept, and crawled under the bed, still clutching her sheet of buttons.

SHE TOLD HER DAUGHTER she was always afraid of the dark when she lived at her cousin's. She used to lie under the bed with her eyes open, not moving until she finally fell asleep. She believed that if she didn't move she would have a better chance of not being noticed. She was afraid of mice, but she liked the slats above her, like the top of a casket. She pretended it was her funeral and how sorry her mother would be.

When she was grown, she sometimes had a dream in which she was lying on the bare ground, not allowed to move. It was of vital importance that she hold perfectly still, because if she moved even the slightest bit, the sun would go out.

ONCE AGAIN THE FAMILY had a house. Franklin Roosevelt was elected, everyone together again. June's mother was thankful to be in a clean place with the church nearby, familiar neighbors, a garden out back, her husband's pay envelope covering the rent again. She was especially thankful to have her youngest daughter June with her again. And so cheerful. The most cheerful girl she could imagine, always laughing and chattering and bringing friends over and going to their houses. That was good, but so different from the little girl she'd had to send away.

June was ebullient, but her mother was weary. Her weariness was such that sometimes she could hardly see. She was frightened because she couldn't see her family as clearly now as she had seen them in her dreams when they were all separated.

She stood at the doorway of her bedroom with the dust mop, amazed by the distance across the linoleum to the four-poster where she had lain through sleepless nights of economic disaster, running her eyes up the posts. Where she had labored for her children. *He* never worried. He worked hard, never drank, always came home at the end of the week and put the money in her hand, asking for just enough back to buy his chewing tobacco. *She* planned how to spend the money, how much to share with the church, how to educate the children. She found herself unexpectedly bitter for how it all fell to her. No wonder her legs were heavy, she thought; it settles through you, drives you down.

She forced the dust mop forward over the linoleum, cabbage rose by cabbage rose. Unsettledness underlay everything like ripples in dark water. How blithely the others picked up their lives. *He* put in a garden before they'd got their furniture back. June gambolled from glee club to church picnic to soda fountain. She worried that June was somehow too light. She attempted moral examples to fit whatever the girl was doing: "You have to consider if it's something Jesus would have done when He was here," she said of a dance. She felt the dark waters stir, grumble; she'd had an easier toouch with her older children.

As she dusted, she found herself reluctant to go too close to the bed. She did not lie down, but she couldn't stop watching the curves of its pillars rising toward the low ceiling of her illness. One day soon, she told herself, I will lie down in that bed for the last time, and the pillars will be flagpoles to heaven. June's mother meant to comfort herself, but instead was frightened— not of dying, but of how little she could imagine the shimmer and delight of heaven.

Years later, June told her own daughter a story about the first time she and her husband went out after the daughter was born. They left the baby with her best friend, June said, and went on a picnic. "I was so ignorant," she said. "You can't imagine how little I knew about babies. I was the baby of my family, you see. When we came back, you were screaming. Since I was nursing you, my friend didn't have any way to feed you."

Her daughter said, "Didn't you think about how the baby would need to nurse?"

June pursed her lips, shook her head. "It's the strangest thing, because I never stopped thinking about you. I had never left you with anyone before, not even for ten minutes. I thought about what you needed every second, if you needed more covers, less covers, to be burped, if the safety pins had come undone. I worried myself sick, I was so afraid of doing the wrong thing. Even at that picnic, I remember talking with the other women about baby things, loose bowels, you know. I never for a second stopped thinking about you."

"Except for that one thing."

"It's very strange," June said.

NOW JUNE'S DAUGHTER is going to have a baby, and she has dreams about passages. In June's daughter's dream, there is a series of cardboard tunnels on a rickety bridge, and they are all too tight for her. The scene changes, and she runs in a squatting position under a tractor trailer, staying low to avoid being crushed. Next, she jogs along a path with other runners ahead and behind her, a cushion of ivy underfoot, a canopy of trees above. The last dream isn't unpleasant, but she still doesn't rest well.

June's daughter says, "I have these dreams because I want to protect my baby. I know I'll protect it from predators and illness, but I worry about lapses and gaps. I worry that I will find myself and the baby in a great flat space with no landmarks or signposts."

June's daughter wonders if it is possible to forgive yourself in advance for what you will certainly do wrong.

Family Knots

NARCISSA FOY MADE patchwork quilts. Even when she was a little girl turning frayed bits of feed sack into covers for her dolls, people praised her neat stitching and nice contrasts of color. After she married and moved over the mountain to live with her husband's family, her fame spread in the new community. She would spend the evenings with her patches spread on the bed, trying to get the colors to move a certain way, until her husband Axel came in yawning dramatically. Most people favored her blue-and-pink Grandma's Flower Garden, but her mother-in-law, Mrs. Foy, preferred a Courthouse Steps pattern in shades of lavender and gray.

Narcissa herself liked the crazy quilts best. Years ago, it was explained to her that a crazy quilt wasn't like a lunatic, but crazed like the cracks under the glaze of old pottery. With a planned quilt, you looked for pieces to play up the pattern, but with a crazy, you went off following trails of color wherever they led and then later discovered the shapes that contained your discovery.

Narcissa didn't say this in so many words: she didn't say much, as a rule, but people noticed her. They liked to look at her with her fine complexion. There was something special about her smile, too, something in her eyes, as if she was always looking partly at you and partly up at the clouds. Then there would be a shift, and just for a second, almost in passing, you would have her eyes in your eyes, all to yourself, and you felt warmed, as if she knew your secret beauty, the part of you that was like the mountains and the clouds.

She was a good girl, too—respectful, quiet, cheerful. She wasn't much of a hand to do fieldwork, but the Foys had plenty of men in those days just before the Great War, and women, too, what with Mrs. Foy's maiden sister and the girls. Narcissa always offered to get up from her quilting to make the cornbread or slop the hogs, but her mother-in-law and the others would say, Sit, sit. When she got pregnant so soon, they were all even more solicitous. They wanted her to feel at home and loved, so far from her own relations.

Some said that Mrs. Foy indulged Narcissa, let her do a young girl's chores too long. She collected the eggs, picked the raspberries, beat an occasional white cake for Sunday dessert, and after the baby came, she sat in the big cane rocker on the porch, sweetly nursing, softly singing, looking up over the hills or down into the baby's eyes.

"Mrs. Foy," she said one afternoon, "I never seen a scrap that color, did you? Wouldn't I love a piece that color."

"What color, honey?" Mrs. Foy was snapping beans and dropping them into the big tin pot where they made a substantial clang.

"Sky eyes," said Narcissa. "The baby's got sky eyes."

Mrs. Foy looked up, not altogether sure what made her so uncomfortable: the rhyme, the hint that Narcissa had strange things going on in her mind? "You mean sky blue, Cissy?"

"No, something different from sky blue. It's a change color."

Mrs. Foy snorted. "Babies' eyes don't settle in for a color till they're right big. I wouldn't worry about it."

"I'm not *worried,* I just wish I had a piece that color. I'd make a quilt called Sky Eyes."

Mrs. Foy winked without meaning to. "I expect you'd have to go to silks for a color like that, and you won't find any silk in this house." But she added, "I have some nice blue lawn in the drawer I was saving. If you want to do some kind of fancy quilt, I'd let you have a little bit of that."

They weren't always comfortable with Narcissa's dreaminess, but in those days she was the kind of luxury a mountain family could afford and even show off with pride. The backbreaking and tedious years of clearing the land and carding the wool to spin the yarn to weave the cloth were over. People worked hard but felt compensated for their labor. There was a design to things that everyone could see, and Narcissa was the touch of red against the blue and tan, the berry in the bush. The juice in the berry. She made the commonplace even more comforting.

But times changed. The girls married and left home and Narcissa had more work and more babies. Mrs. Foy and Aunt got older. Narcissa's skin lost some of its resilience and color, and the subtle thinning of her lips made her look more capable of work, whatever she felt inside. She always did what was asked of her, but she managed to keep on making her quilts. When Mrs. Foy complained about the time she spent on her quilts, Narcissa turned out to have the jaw of a bull terrier. She hung on to what mattered to her. It didn't make her sweeter to bite in so grimly, but it made quilts.

Maybe it would have been better if Narcissa had been born a few years later. Maybe it wasn't really quilts she wanted to make. Maybe in another time she would have been a painter, or a performance artist, a field scientist who studied wild pygmy chimpanzees, or the discoverer of the genes that cause the variations in Indian corn. Or perhaps she would have accomplished more with her quilts if she'd borne fewer children. Her fourth labor was fierce; the baby was breech and nearly strangled by the cord, but they saved it, and it immediately grew large and voracious, a night screamer and nipple chomper who nursed for hours at a time. Narcissa's breasts became caked and inflamed, and she cried and whimpered along with the baby, who seemed to thrive on blood as on milk.

The family had no time to sit and hold her hand. They knew it was difficult, but so was harvest season. And, if the truth be told, Mrs. Foy and Aunt, and even Axel, secretly thought that they wouldn't mind a little fever and infection themselves if it meant they could sit on the porch in the overheated beauty of the late afternoons, with the mountains rising directly behind, unutterably green with buzzing and enormous thunderheads in the west and blue. When she had a moment's respite, Narcissa looked up and groaned at the beauty. When the baby rested from its gobbling and gumming, she fell into a feverish nap and dreamed of quadrants of green and lavender, some milky, some bloody, and a ground the color of baby flesh. She dreamed of a quilt the color of her struggle to nourish this baby and the color of the peace she couldn't get hold of. The colors began to trickle and form paths like veins, twisting, weaving, plaiding, bursting open like fireworks or zinnia petals unfurled.

The fever of her inflamed breasts broke with the firework zinnia and the storm. It's not a crazy quilt at all, she thought, watching the sheets of gray rain slash at the hillside, watching the old women hurry in the wash. I'll have to make up some fool name for it, I'll call it the Exploding Zinnia or Shriek of the Wild Cat, just so they'll know it's a pattern and then I can do whatever I want with it.

The quilt should have been a new beginning, a breakthrough. She was all ready to start on it, but then the one thing happened that nobody expected. And Narcissa saw that *this* was a pattern too, the inevitability of the unexpected. Aunt—Mrs. Foy's sister, the maiden, spinster, scrawny fifty-year-old with a stoop— revealed that she had a secret beau and was going to marry him and go live in town. It made Narcissa's peculiarities pale. Aunt asked Narcissa for a red, white, and blue Star of Bethlehem quilt, and Narcissa made the most beautiful one ever, the one that her oldest daughter Lou eventually inherited.

And then Mrs. Foy went to bed with dropsy, her legs swollen and propped on pillows. Narcissa took a step back, saw: Aunt gone; Mrs. Foy in bed; Lou supposed to be free to do her homework because she was so smart; and the men waiting for their dinner. A headache struck the back of her eyes like a blow. This was an old story—the sudden, the unexpected, the demands of living. Narcissa was now the one to start the fire in the morning and set the biscuits to rise. Narcissa to boil the great kettle on Monday morning for the wash, to make pistons of her arms over the washboard. Narcissa to run to the big bedroom and help Mrs. Foy with the chamber pot. Her headache ended, but it was followed by the toothache, and she lost four teeth and whatever was left of the sweetness that used to make people forgive her oddities. She never went bitter about the mouth, but she sealed off something in herself the way Brother's left thigh sealed off a piece of shrapnel. Brother came back from the Great War alive and walking, thank the good Lord, with just a slight limp, but there was a piece of metal in him all the same, and on certain days, he could feel its weight. Thus Narcissa—her quilt.

One day she saw a spider weaving its web in a corner of her quilting frame. It was a beautiful web of exquisite, complex design, and she ripped it apart and rubbed it into the grain of the wall boards.

"You told us spiders eat flies," said Lou, who was supposed to be studying. "You told us spiders do good."

"It was in my frame," said Narcissa. "I was jealous of that spider's web."

That night she prayed for forgiveness for killing the spider. She prayed for strength, and received just enough to stay awake and start piecing the exploding zinnia. What God gave her to see was that if she was going to make that quilt for love or money or glory-be, she had better make it now, because there was no slack time coming. She had the extra bit of energy every night, and sometimes in the day.

Once, she was working on the quilt and didn't get to the tomatoes until they were so heavy they dropped to the ground and
rotted. Mrs. Foy couldn't get over it and counted up the number
of lost quarts. "It's that quilt, Narcissa," she said. "You're using
such little small pieces. It'll take too long to finish."

Narcissa's bull terrier clamped shut. "Mrs. Foy, I'm real sorry,
but I have to say, it's only tomatoes. I don't think a peck of tomatoes is all that's standing between this family and starvation."

She had never talked back to Mrs. Foy before, and Mrs. Foy,
who didn't know how to take it, had an uncomfortable feeling
that it was a bad sign.

"It's the waste, Narcissa," she said. "You know very well it's the
waste that bothers me. Just the same as with that quilt. I swear
that quilt is going to take forever, Narcissa. All of them say it just
has too many pieces."

Narcissa kept her jaw tight. "I'm not making this quilt for all
of them. I'm making this quilt—I'm making this quilt—" and she
wasn't going to say it was for herself, although it was, because it
was also for the family and the neighbors, "I'm making this one
for God," she said.

Mrs. Foy snorted and shook her head and said to herself: That
Narcissa. That's just like Narcissa. Make a quilt for God. What's
she going to do, hang it at church? Mrs. Foy decided then and
there she had really better get out of bed and take charge if they
were going to have anything put up for winter.

When the quilt was finished, Narcissa decided it wasn't a
flower after all. It didn't satisfy her with its dark complexities.
Where was that fleshy life color she had wanted? The shapes
were crude, the color changes too quick and uneven. People

called it unusual. Narcissa called it Family Knots and folded it away in the cedar chest, and started in on some bright cheerful ones that refreshed her spirit. She continued to make up her own patterns, though, including a nice one called Big Zinnia with new cloth Axel bought her as a present.

The cheerful quilt ushered in a good period. Mrs. Foy was better, the boys came back from overseas, and Narcissa got pregnant again. This time it didn't seem like such a burden, though, because they'd sold off the coal and timber rights and used the money for a new washing machine. They stopped baking bread, too, and bought white bread at the store, and sometimes pies in boxes. Lou did more around the house, usually with a book stuck in her apron. She had always been quick with words. And right before the baby was born, Narcissa sold Big Zinnia to some city people for an astounding sum of money.

Some other city people came another time to look at Narcissa's quilts and asked why she didn't do more of the traditional patterns. "Such beautiful work," they said. "So colorful, but what about Dutch Girl and Barn Door? Don't you ever do a Honeycomb or a Bear's Paw or Virginia Reel or Country Squares?"

And before Narcissa could answer, Lou jumped in. "Why," she said, "Don't you reckanize that pattern? All my mama's patterns go back to the American Revolution. That one there is called the General George Washington Dancing Quilt."

Actually it was called Canning Beans Is Hard Work, and she should have shamed Lou for telling people stories, but the city people said, Oh, they hadn't seen it right off, of course it was, and offered her too much money. She took it and mentally changed the quilt's name to save Lou from lying. It could just as easy be called General George Washington Dancing, she thought.

Mrs. Foy was in bed again. "I'm getting too old, Narcissa," she said. "You must start taking over, planning the things."

Well, Narcissa had been planning everything for five years now. "I will, Mrs. Foy," she said, "but you know it won't be the way you do things."

She had meant to pay the older woman a compliment, but tears popped out in Mrs. Foy's eyes. "That's hard, Narcissa Foy," she said. "That's a hard thing for a woman to hear. The day will come when Lou will spit in your face too." But then Mrs. Foy seemed to come to herself. "Now Narcissa," she said. "I never meant anything. You know we all love you like a daughter. We always did. We spoiled you a little in the beginning, but you worked out just fine." She looked out the window and patted Narcissa's hand.

Once, during Mrs. Foy's final illness, Narcissa took out the strange dark quilt called Family Knots and nailed it to a pine strip and hung it in the hall. Axel said, "What's that thing doing on the wall?" And then got so busy sniffing around the kitchen for his dinner he forgot to wait for an answer. Or maybe didn't need an answer, just wanted Narcissa to know he noticed.

Mrs. Foy noticed too, tossed on her pillow and moaned. "You're still trying to convince me you don't have sense to run a house, but I know better, Narcissa, I know better."

Narcissa sat down and followed the complicated flow of Family Knots under bridges and over rapids. She recalled that as she was working on it, she had named the prominent navy blue stream Mother and a series of broken loops in green and brown Father. A deep maroon was Sweetheart Love, and Little Girl and Baby Boy burst out here and there in bright splashes.

Then she went through her chest and found a very old crazy that she had made when she was young, all in robin's egg blue and yellow, and she nailed that one to a pine strip and hung it up too. She was looking for something she had lost or put away. Every few days she would sit down and study those quilts, but when Mrs. Foy died, out of respect, she took them off the wall and laid her out in her favorite, the old lavender Courthouse Steps.

The day after the funeral, she started on the best quilt of her life. It was a variation on Family Knots, somewhat simplified but using sixty different brown and tans and thirty blues and thirty violets and purples. Unlike the first Family Knots, it had no background proper; everything was foreground, all equal. She called it—feeling fancy because she knew it was a success—Braided Candelabra, even though it was really another Family Knots. She took great satisfaction in that quilt; she laid it on her and Axel's bed and never would consider an offer for it.

After that, her quilts were fewer, but just what she meant them to be, and they took a place in her life as if each of them were a child of hers, or at least a niece or nephew.

Mrs. Foy's boys married and left, and Narcissa and Axel's boys grew big and healthy. Lou became either a schoolteacher or a flapper, it was hard to tell from the way she dressed when she came for a visit. She was taking art courses in the evenings, and she came back with her red mouth going a mile a minute. Why didn't Narcissa realize that *she* was the artist? said Lou. These weren't quilts, these were easel paintings in cloth. Narcissa had all on her own invented Dynamism and the Fauves, said Lou.

"What's Fauves?" said Axel. "Sounds like some kind of purple fox to me," and they all had a laugh, but Narcissa was interested and flattered, and she trusted that in the end Lou would separate out the wheat from the chaff. It was too much, though, when Lou told her to drop everything and come back to the city with her and study at the Art School. "Now Lou," said Narcissa. "Now Lou," as if Lou had told an off-color story.

"It will smother your talent, never leaving here," insisted Lou. "It will just smother you."

Narcissa wondered if she *had* been smothered, and allowed it was possible that something had been, but something else had been made strong. She remembered the baby who chewed her nipples, but couldn't remember which one it was, and she remembered poring over the quilt pieces by kerosene lantern till they burnt into her eyes. She remembered a time when she used to be in her own world and it surprised her when dinner appeared on the table. She remembered, too, that a time had come when they began to touch her, Axel first, then his brothers and sisters and her own babies and, finally, even the old people. And I began to hear them and speak back, Narcissa thought, as if she were telling her own story. And after that, quilts weren't the most important thing anymore, or rather, everything wasn't separate from the quilts. It was the quilts, Narcissa thought, *and* the family. The pattern of people, and I was in the pattern.

About the Author

Photo by Andrew B. Weinberger

MEREDITH SUE WILLIS was raised in Shinnston, West Virginia. Growing up in an atmosphere of story telling, preaching, and radio melodramas, she published her first story when she was fifteen years old. She dropped out of college to become a VISTA volunteer—the subject of her novel *Only Great Changes*. After VISTA, she returned to college to continue her literary interests, but worked equally hard protesting the Vietnam War. She was a member of the Students for a Democratic Society and a participant in the 1968 sit-ins at Columbia University, where she earned her MFA degree.

She worked as a writer-in-the-schools with Teachers & Writers Collaborative, which publishes her books on creative writing: *Personal Fiction Writing, Blazing Pencils,* and *Deep Revision.* Her other published work includes *A Space Apart, Higher Ground, Only Great Changes, Quilt Pieces,* and a novel for children, *The Secret Super Powers of Marco.*

Willis has lived for twenty years in and around New York City. A veteran teacher of writing workshops for children and adults, she has taught at New York University, Kean College, Cooper Union, Pace University, and Pratt Institute. She is a two-time winner of the PEN Syndicated Fiction Contest as well as the recipient of literary fellowships from the National Endowment for the Arts and the New Jersey State Council on the Arts. She lives in South Orange, New Jersey, with her husband, Andrew Weinberger, and son, Joel.